Written and illustrated by

ROB BIDDULPH

MACMILLAN CHILDREN'S BOOKS

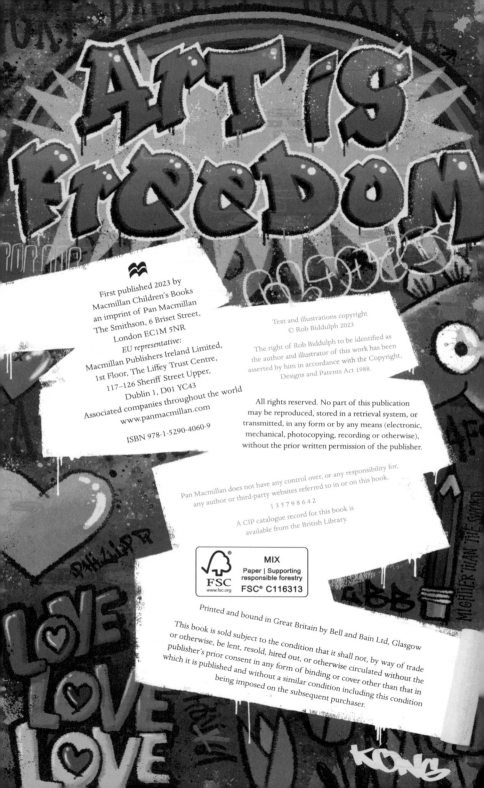

First published 2023 by
Macmillan Children's Books
an imprint of Pan Macmillan
The Smithson, 6 Briset Street,
London EC1M 5NR
EU representative:
Macmillan Publishers Ireland Limited,
1st Floor, The Liffey Trust Centre,
117–126 Sheriff Street Upper,
Dublin 1, D01 YC43
Associated companies throughout the world
www.panmacmillan.com

ISBN 978-1-5290-4060-9

Text and illustrations copyright
© Rob Biddulph 2023

The right of Rob Biddulph to be identified as
the author and illustrator of this work has been
asserted by him in accordance with the Copyright,
Designs and Patents Act 1988.

Pan Macmillan does not have any control over, or any responsibility for,
any author or third-party websites referred to in or on this book.

1 3 5 7 9 8 6 4 2

A CIP catalogue record for this book is
available from the British Library.

MIX
Paper | Supporting
responsible forestry
FSC® C116313
FSC www.fsc.org

Printed and bound in Great Britain by Bell and Bain Ltd, Glasgow

For Sarah,

who steered the ship

Prologue

Mr White's eyes narrowed as the curtain began to fall.

On the stage, *Swan Lake*'s prima ballerina looked exhausted as she took in the enthusiastic applause of the audience. Playing the dual roles of Odette, the beautiful swan princess, and Odile, the scheming black swan, was a huge undertaking. It had, no doubt, required incredible amounts of concentration and focus. White knew how the dancer felt. He had been playing two different parts for such a long time; keeping them separate had been difficult and, at times, draining. Oh well. At least he wouldn't have to do it for much longer. The endgame was in sight.

White looked at his two companions and shook his head. *Fools*, he thought. *They're totally oblivious to the real reason we've come to see this ridiculous performance.* He smiled. *Not long now, though, until it all becomes painfully clear. It's only a matter of time until SHE turns up, with her simpering little friends in tow. Then, at last, the final stages of my plan can play out, and these two imbeciles will have served their purpose.*

He reached up and adjusted his hat.

The blonde lady turned to face him. 'Wasn't that FANTASTIC?' she said, her eyes still wide with excitement.

'I'm not going to lie to you, I absolutely loved it,' replied the Welsh woman, the enthusiasm in her voice taking White by surprise. 'But we'd best get back to the hotel sharpish. We have an early start in the morning. I've booked us a private view of da Vinci's *The Last Supper* at that little church around the corner, but we need to be there before the crowds turn up. It's cost you a lot more than thirty pieces of silver, Mr Stone, so we should make sure you get your money's worth.'

He grunted and nodded his approval.

'Right then, let's go, lovelies,' continued Nerys. 'I've got a feeling that tomorrow is going to be a busy day.'

Part One

...in which Peanut
attempts a daring rescue

1
Going Underground

hey walked, at pace, down a long, metal-lined corridor. Gary Jones led the way, followed by his daughter Peanut, her younger sister Little-Bit, their older brother Leo, and Peanut's friend, Rockwell Riley. Woodhouse, a talking rat with a strong Glaswegian accent, and 67, a large silver robot who had recently defected from the city's RAZER army, brought up the rear. Rockwell was trying to stay as far away from the rat as possible, but it was proving difficult in the narrow corridor.

'Whoa! So many books,' said Little-Bit, looking to her left at the packed shelves that ran the entire length of the wall. 'What are they all about, Daddy?'

'Chroma, mainly,' he replied. 'Woodhouse and 67 sourced them for me. I thought I should be productive with my time while hidden away and learn as much as I could about the place and its history. I have spent a lot of time here, after all. The books were also a good distraction. I was missing you all so much.' He pulled Little-Bit in for a quick hug.

A few months ago, Dad had escaped from the Spire, a huge tower in the middle of the Illustrated City which, until very recently, had been serving as a prison for enemies of Chroma's evil mayor, Mr White. Although Dad had been imprisoned for many years, time moved at a much faster rate in Chroma. So, as far as his children were concerned, he had only been missing for a little over twelve months. That was more than long enough, however.

A few days after he'd disappeared from home, a postcard had arrived at the Jones's house, supposedly from Dad. It said that he had left the family and gone to live in Mexico. But Peanut hadn't believed a word of it. Not for one second. She *knew* that her dad would never leave them, and she had been very vocal about the fact. However, Peanut's mother, Tracey Jones, had taken the postcard at face value and was furious with her husband for deserting them all.

Now that Peanut had been proved right, she couldn't wait to give her mother the good news: that Dad *hadn't* left them. Instead, he'd been kidnapped and imprisoned inside a tower at the centre of an illustrated city in another dimension by Mr White, who, incidentally, was the alter ego of Mr Stone, her boss at the accountancy firm.

Peanut sighed. She realised how far-fetched it sounded. But it *was* true and Mum needed to know that truth as soon as possible – especially as she was currently with Mr Stone in Milan and, Peanut believed, in serious trouble.

'Let's pick up the

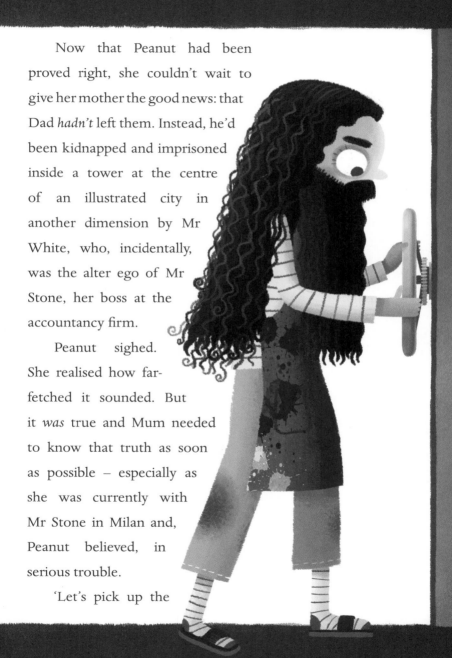

pace,' Dad said gently but with determination in his voice. 'It's important we get to Italy as soon as possible to rescue your mum.'

Knowing how dangerous Mr Stone was, Peanut was glad that Dad had come up with a plan so quickly.

The group finally reached the door at the end of the corridor and Dad turned the large, metal wheel that was attached to it. It made a strange hissing sound as it rotated. Once he had unlocked it, Dad opened the heavy door and ushered everyone into a small, windowless room. He shut the door behind them with a loud clang, locked it via another large wheel, and told 67 to press the button on the wall. The whole room juddered, and then slowly began to move downwards.

'Ooh, a lift,' said Rockwell. 'Where is it taking us?'

'Och, you'll see, pal,' said Woodhouse the rat. 'You'll see.'

2
The Component Parts

Peanut turned to her father and smiled as they descended. 'So, you're definitely Conté's heir, then?' she asked.

Nicolas-Jacques Conté was a famous French engineer credited with inventing the pencil in the late eighteenth century. His prototype, Pencil Number One, also known as Little Tail, was currently sitting snugly in Peanut's bandolier, the shoulder belt in which she kept her art materials.

It was this pencil's magical properties – the fact that whatever it draws becomes real – that had brought Peanut and her friends to Chroma in the first place when she had sketched a door in her bedroom and walked through it. This portal-creating ability was unique to the pencil, and therefore made it something that Mr White desperately wanted. He'd stolen it from Peanut during her first adventure in Chroma, but luckily she'd managed to get it back. She still couldn't quite believe that Dad, her free-spirited artist of a father, was Conté's heir. On the other hand, she totally believed it. He *was* something of an artistic genius, after all.

'Well, the Markmakers seem to think so,' replied Dad. Millicent and Malcolm Markmaker were the leaders of Chroma's Resistance army, the one that Peanut, Rockwell and Little-Bit had just helped to reclaim control of the city. 'And, apparently, so does Mr White. Our intelligence tells us that I've been his primary target ever since he discovered that Pencil Number One existed. It's probably because he thinks I'm the heir and he knows what the heir can do with the pencil. That's why I had to stay in hiding during the Battle for the Spire. So that White wasn't able to capture me.'

'If he had, we would have just rescued you,' said Little-Bit, confidently.

'I'm sure you would have tried your best,' said Dad with a smile, 'but, quite frankly, I don't think White would have kept me rescuable for too long, if you know what I mean. I think he wants to see the back of Conté's heir once and for all.'

Peanut, Little-Bit and Leo went white at the thought.

'Oh, don't worry, kids,' said Dad quickly, seeing their frightened faces. 'I won't let him hurt me. And now that I have you guys here to protect me, I feel as safe as houses.'

The colour began to return to their cheeks.

The lift came to an abrupt stop and Dad flicked a switch to the right of the door. A small screen lit up showing grainy black-and-white footage of another room, which appeared to be completely filled with water. He then flicked a second switch and the liquid began to drain away.

'Why's this Mr White bloke so worried about Conté's heir, anyway?' asked Leo.

'Well, if the Markmakers and all of those history books are right,' said Dad, 'when Conté's heir holds Pencil Number One in their hand, an unbelievably potent magic force is released. This force would immediately restore all of the creative power that the city once had, that which Mr White has spent so long trying to destroy. As such, the pencil – *that* pencil,' he nodded towards Peanut's bandolier, 'could well be the most powerful weapon we have against White and his plan to destroy Chroma. And now that you've got Little Tail back, it's even more important that I stay hidden. We're so close to ending this. We just need to keep both component parts of the

weapon safe until we have captured
White. Those component parts
being Pencil Number One
and me.'

'Hang on,' said Rockwell. 'Why can't we just
give you Little Tail now? Wouldn't that instantly sort
everything out?'

'It's tempting,' said Dad. 'But it's too much of a risk. I want
to make sure that White is captured and, more importantly,
that Mum is safe before we do anything with the pencil.
There's so much uncertainty right now.'

Peanut pulled Little Tail from its special slot in her
bandolier and looked at it. It felt much heavier than an object
of that size should feel.

'Such a small thing,' she whispered, 'but so important.
Are you sure you don't want to take it now?' She held it out,
offering it to her father.

His eyes widened, and he swallowed loudly. He began to
lift his hand, but quickly dropped it back to his side.

'No,' he said. 'Not until White is safely locked up. Nobody knows for sure how the magic works and, as the Markmakers are always saying, we might only have one shot at this. We have to make sure we do it properly.'

3
The Airlock

Once all of the water in the room on the screen had drained away, Dad started turning the wheel to open the door. Again, this brought with it a soft hissing sound. They walked into an even smaller metal room with a round hatch at the opposite end – it was the same one they'd seen on the screen and the floor was still wet. Once they were all crammed inside, 67 shut the door they'd just come through and pressed a button on the wall. More hissing.

'Ah, it's an airlock,' said Rockwell. 'Astronauts use them. I think it has something to do with getting them used to being out in proper space after they've been sitting in a nice comfy spaceship for ages.'

'That is incorrect,' said 67. 'Everybody, please disregard

what the Tall Human just said. He is displaying an extraordinary lack of knowledge.'

'Whoa!' said an astonished Rockwell. 'That's a bit harsh isn't it? OK, if it's not an airlock what is it then, Einstein?'

'Actually, my name is 67. I am a second-generation RAZER designed by Josephine Engelberger of Chroma. Albert Einstein was a theoretical physicist best known for his work in the

field of quantum physics and, in particular, for developing the theory of relativity and the mass-energy equivalence formula $E = mc^2$. It should be clear to anybody with fully functioning cognitive facility that we are not one and the same being.' The robot turned to face Dad. 'Gary Jones, I suspect that the Tall Human is considerably less intelligent than he thinks he is.'

'Is he being serious?' asked a flabbergasted Rockwell, looking at Peanut for back-up. She shrugged her shoulders.

'I am not a "he",' said 67, facing Rockwell again. 'RAZERs are not given a pre-assigned gender. My pronouns are they/them.'

'Oh,' said Rockwell. 'Well, I'm sorry. I didn't mean to—'

'Apology not accepted,' interrupted 67. Rockwell's jaw dropped. 'Anyway, we are not currently in space, as should be obvious to anyone with a modicum of common sense. We are, in fact, far below the water table and about to enter a sub-aqua environment. As such, certain precautions must be taken regarding air pressure. It needs to be equalised via a decompression sequence. That is to say, it must be adjusted until the pressure in the current chamber matches the pressure in the destination chamber. I will concede that it bears certain similarities to astronautical airlock systems, but on the most fundamental level it is quite different. It really is very simple to understand, even for a being with a limited capacity for assimilating information like Tall Human, here.'

'Yeah, Tall Human,' said a giggling Little-Bit. 'Maybe next time you'll think before you speak.'

4
The Submarine

Once the hissing noise had stopped, Dad opened the round hatch and ushered everyone through. This room was quite different to the others – longer and narrower, with a retro feel to it, like the interior of a spaceship on a 1960s TV show. Most of the room was nickel-plated and festooned with visible rivets, gleaming pipework and round gauges with needles that turned very slowly. The children looked around with shiny, curious eyes.

'How cool,' said Little-Bit as she surveyed the tube-shaped interior. 'It reminds me of being on the London Underground, except that the windows are smaller and there aren't as many copies of the *Evening Standard* strewn across the floor.'

'Hang on, is that water?' said Peanut, looking out through

one of the portholes that lined each side of the room. 'Are we in a submarine?'

'We certainly are, lassie,' replied Woodhouse. 'Us rats usually prefer to flee sinking ships, so it always feels strange to be getting into one voluntarily.'

'Are we in the Rainbow Lake?' asked Rockwell. 'Look at all the different colours!'

Sure enough, the vessel's interior was bathed in the kaleidoscope of undulating light that was coming in through the windows. Every porthole provided a different-coloured view.

The Rainbow Lake was the magical body of water that surrounded the Spire in the very centre of Chroma. Everybody who swam in it was imbued with an amazing sense of creativity. It was said that all of the great artists throughout history had, at some point, swum in the lake before going on to produce their wonderful works of art. It was widely regarded as the hub of all the world's creativity.

MODERNIA CLEANING STATION

'Not exactly,' said Dad, replying to Rockwell. 'But you're very close. We are in the Rainbow Lake's cleaning channel.' He pointed out several large propellor-shaped devices attached to the outside of the submarine. 'You see those filter wheels? They clean the water and help with colour correction.'

'I think I remember someone mentioning colour correction at some point,' said Peanut. 'But why does the water need to be cleaned? I thought it was magical.'

'It does have many magical properties, yes, but in order to remain potent, the water needs to be in tip-top condition,' Dad explained. 'That's why it's regularly circulated through

these channels and carefully treated so that it's always perfect. At least, that's what *should* happen. The truth is that the cleaning programme hasn't been operating for a long time. As you can see, most of the equipment is pretty neglected and much of the water is now stagnant.'

The children looked through the window and, sure enough, some of the filter wheels on the side of the sub were rusty. A few even had blades missing. Peanut noticed another submarine resting on its side on the channel bed, dented and dirty.

'Despite its current condition, I'm always surprised at how beautiful the rainbow water is,' said Dad as he gazed at the slowly moving, constantly shape-shifting pockets of colour outside the vessel. 'It's like being inside the most beautiful lava lamp ever. And I can't tell you how wonderful it is to be sharing a bit of this beauty with you all, even if the circumstances aren't ideal. I've been looking at this on my own for so long. The bright colours always reminded me of you, Peanut.'

Dad smiled back, then looked up towards the surface of the water. 'All that being said, the levels are getting really low now. It's worrying. On the plus side, the fact that nobody's monitoring the channels means that we can use them to travel around the city without being seen.'

'Is the water from the Rainbow Lake taken all around Chroma?' asked Peanut.

'Not *all* around Chroma, just the south-western part of it. The dirty water is diverted from the Rainbow Lake and

funnelled south, down a long, straight underground waterway, to the outskirts of the city. That's where we are now – the cleaning station just outside of Modernia. It's then pumped clockwise around the perimeter of Chroma until it reaches the station on the outskirts of the Green Valleys, at which point it turns and heads east along another channel until, eventually, it re-joins the lake. By then, it's usually all sparkly and fully

'Ingenious,' said Little-Bit. 'So the water is cleaned by the various filtering systems, one of which is a fleet of submarines just like this one?'

'Yes,' replied Dad. 'And because it's a constant process, *all* of the water in the lake is perfect *all* of the time. At least it would be if the system was operating properly.'

'How did it get to be in such a terrible state?' asked Rockwell.

'It has been totally neglected since Mr White became mayor,' said Dad. 'Let's just say maintaining the colour quality of the Rainbow Lake so that it remains a creative resource has *not* been high on his priority list. Fortunately, I was able to get this submarine working again – 67 was a big help in that regard, of course.'

Rockwell glanced over at the robot, who didn't return his gaze.

'Anyway, we'd better get a shift on,' said Dad.

He walked to the opposite end of the submarine and took a seat behind two large joysticks, a busy-looking control panel and an enormous periscope. He pressed a few buttons, flicked a couple of switches and then turned a silver ignition key. The engines immediately fired, creating an explosion of tiny bubbles in the water surrounding the vessel. Peanut gazed at them through the window. They echoed the nervous bubbles of energy she could feel in her tummy.

'We need to get moving,' said Dad, pulling the periscope's eyepiece towards him. 'The more time we waste, the more danger Mum is in.'

He pushed the left joystick. The submarine lurched forward and began cutting through the rainbow-coloured water at a slow, but steady, speed.

'Leo, Peanut, Little-Bit,' said Dad, 'let's go and rescue your mother.'

5

67's Story

The children looked out of the portholes, marvelling as the submarine moved through the water.

'These fish are BONKERS,' said Little-Bit, referring to the myriad of creatures that lived in the cleaning channel. 'That one looks like a Christmas tree and I swear I just saw a jellyfish that could easily pass as a trifle. It actually made me feel a bit peckish.'

'Does anyone know what time it is?' shouted Dad from behind the periscope at the front of the sub.

Peanut looked at her watch. 'Oh, it's stopped working,' she said.

'A common occurrence when a person is crossing between dimensions,' said 67 matter-of-factly. 'Especially those which operate at different time rates. I assume your timepiece is a harmonic oscillator, which means that the inertia of the balance wheel and the elasticity of the balance spring have probably been subject to too much change. Only the very best movements are

able to withstand such trauma over a sustained period, and I would guess that your watch features neither a Rolex calibre 3235 or a Lemania 2310, regardless of whether or not a coaxial escapement is included.'

'Er, I think what the robot is trying to say is that all of

this travelling between Chroma and London has busted your watch,' said Rockwell. 'Give it here and I'll take a look. I've read a couple of engineering books that covered basic watchmaking. I reckon I might be able to fix it.'

Peanut removed the watch and handed it to her friend.

'I wouldn't let Tall Human get your hopes up if I were you, Peanut Jones,' said 67, much to Rockwell's annoyance. 'And to answer your question, Gary Jones, the time here in Chroma is 1804 hours.'

'That means it's probably still yesterday in Milan,' Dad reckoned, pushing the left joystick further forward. 'This old girl is pretty slow, but she should get us to the Green Valleys in time.'

'Why are we going to the Green Valleys?' asked Peanut.

'I'll explain everything a bit later, I promise,' replied Dad. 'In the meantime, you lot should try to get some rest. You're going to need as much energy as possible.'

'Er, 67,' said Little-Bit quietly as she sat next to where the robot was hovering, 'can I ask you a question? Why did you betray Mr White? What made you decide to help our dad? And how did you get him out of prison?'

'Technically, you have asked me four questions, Small Human,' replied the robot. 'I am, however, happy to answer

them all. I am a second-generation RAZER –
a considerable upgrade on the launch model.
We have been given more autonomy by the
programmers. This means we can
make our own decisions. We
have the ability to weigh up a
situation and act as we see fit
with no need for instruction. So,
when I saw what was happening
to Chroma and its citizens,
I made a decision to act.'

'That's exactly what 72 said to us in Die Brücke,' noted
Peanut, who had been eavesdropping from the bench on the
other side of the submarine.

'What is 72?' asked 67.

'The only other RAZER we've ever met,' replied Peanut.
'A really good robot. I miss them.'

'Understood,' said 67, who, to Peanut and Little-Bit's
surprise, didn't seem to want to know more. 'To continue,
I was aware that your father, Gary Jones, was Mr White's
most prized detainee. As such, he was being held in one of
the maximum-security cells near the top of the Spire. That's
where the most valuable enemies of the city were imprisoned.
I decided I would make it my goal to free him.'

'Oh, wow,' said Little-Bit. 'And did the Markmakers

help you like they helped 72? Are you an agent of the Resistance too?'

'Negative,' replied 67. 'I acted alone.'

'So how did you manage to get Dad out?' asked Leo, who had been listening in and was pretty interested to hear how a robot had rescued his father.

'I formulated an ingenious plan which I then executed over a number of months. It involved a fire extinguisher, the water in the Rainbow Lake, a waste pipe and the cleaning channels.'

'Go on . . .' said Peanut and Little-Bit together.

'Mr White had been draining water from the Rainbow Lake for a long time. He had a small amount pumped to the top of the Spire which he used to fill his own personal Rainbow Pool, located just below the control room. I believe his plan was to empty the lake slowly while keeping a supply for his sole use. As such, there was a comprehensive network of pumps and pipes between the lake and the top floor of the tower.'

'That explains the water that Rockwell and I saw when we lifted the hatch in the control room with all the doors,' exclaimed Peanut, remembering the last time they had visited the Spire.

At the sound of his name, Rockwell

looked up from his seat a few metres away and began to listen more closely.

'Indeed,' continued 67. 'I determined fairly early on that as well as the pipes taking water up to Mr White's pool, there was also one that took a little back down to the lake so that his supply could be circulated through the cleaning and colour-correction systems. Even though the systems weren't functioning brilliantly, they were still quite effective on small amounts of water. The pipe that took his water was built into the cavity between the outer and inner walls like the others. But *unlike* the others, it descended in a spiral so that the speed of the water could be controlled. This fact, I realised, meant that it would be safe for a human to travel inside of it.'

'Ooh, so it was kind of like a giant water slide crossed with a helter-skelter?' said an excited Little-Bit.

'Affirmative. That is a very accurate description, Small Human,' replied the robot.

'So, all you needed to do was get Dad into the pipe?' said Leo.

'Affirmative,' said 67. 'And that was relatively easy. All prisoners were permitted ten minutes of exercise per day. For those in the maximum-security unit, that exercise involved walking two laps of the corridor connecting the cells, accompanied by a RAZER, of course. All I had to do was secure a position on exercise detail, convince Gary Jones of my intentions to rescue him, explain my plan and get him to agree to partake.'

'So how did you get him into the pipe?' asked Little-Bit.

'That part was simple. I secured a maintenance detail on the top floor, and then, while pretending to fix some circuitry in one of the wall-mounted communications panels, I fashioned a large opening in said wall, which I subsequently disguised as a fire extinguisher point. Then, during the very next exercise session, when we passed the fire extinguisher, Gary Jones opened the hatch, climbed into the pipe and rode the flume of dirty rainbow water all the way down into the Rainbow Lake. He then swam as fast as he could towards the cleaning channel, the one that runs due south, and then on to the cleaning station outside of Modernia. It would prove to be a long and arduous journey for Gary Jones, but one that he managed to complete successfully.'

'I couldn't have done it without you,' shouted Dad from his position at the front of the submarine. 'You're a real hero, 67. And a true friend.'

The robot's eyes momentarily flicked from green to red. It was almost like they were blushing.

'And then you met up with Dad at the Modernia station?' asked Peanut.

'Affirmative,' said the robot. 'And that's also where we met the rat.'

6
Woodhouse's Story

Peanut, Little-Bit, Leo and Rockwell all turned to look at Woodhouse. He had climbed up onto one of the benches and was looking out of a porthole. As he turned to face them, his long, thick tail – which seemed to have a mind of its own – arranged itself neatly in a circle around him.

Rockwell did his best to conceal a shudder.

'So how did *you* end up joining the Resistance, Woodhouse?' asked Peanut, looking at the rat fondly. Unlike Rockwell, she'd always rather liked small, furry animals. Particularly ones that had helped to rescue her father.

'Well, it's a long story and not a very happy one, I'm afraid,' replied the rat.

'We've got time,' said Peanut, looking out at the coloured water moving slowly past the portholes. 'Dad says it'll take all night to get to the Green Valleys.'

'That's true, lassie,' replied Woodhouse. 'But you really should be getting some rest.'

'Oh, pleeeeeease,' said Little-Bit, plaintively.

'OK,' sighed Woodhouse. 'If I must.'

He jumped down from the bench, tail following him, and stood on his hind legs in the middle of the submarine. He assumed the pose of a Shakespearian actor about to deliver a soliloquy.

'My family have lived in Chroma for generations,' he began. 'Believe it or not, we come from a long line of very noble illustrated rats. The first Woodhouses were drawn by William MacGillivray, the famous eighteenth-century Scottish naturalist, when he visited Chroma as a young man. It's something we've always been very proud of. We're practically rodent royalty.' He picked up his tail and coiled the end into a crown shape which he rested on his head.

'My ancestors settled in Warholia and that's where we've remained. Braw rat country, is Warholia. Plenty of water, plenty of food. Lots of nooks and crannies in which we can ply our trade. Most of us are graffiti artists, y'see. We like to work under cover of darkness and brighten up little corners of the city with our art, in areas otherwise ignored by creatives.

Many Warholian alleyways feature my tag. I've done my fair share of modelling for other graffiti artists too. One time, I posed on a deckchair wearing a pair of sunglasses for a visiting chap who made many stencils based on my likeness. Banksy, I think his name was.'

'So, what made you want to rise up against Mr White?' asked Peanut.

'The Great Whitewash, that's what,' said the rat.

'Er, what was the Great Whitewash?' asked Leo.

'I think I remember Josephine Engelberger saying something about that,' said Peanut. 'Mr White got his RAZERs to paint over the beautiful artwork decorating the walls of Warholia, didn't he?'

'Aye. All that amazing colour,' said Woodhouse, shaking his head. 'Gone in a matter of hours. He also outlawed graffiti. Suddenly, my family and I were lost. Our entire mode of creativity had been taken away from us. That was when

I knew I had to do something.'

'So, what did you do?' asked Little-Bit.

'Well, it took a while, but eventually a friend of mine put me in touch with someone she knew in the Resistance. Within a week, I was standing in a room with the great Mrs Markmaker. That's when she told me about . . . the job.'

'The job? What job?' asked Peanut.

'I know what job,' said Leo. 'Delivering Post-it notes to the National Portrait Gallery.'

'Aye, laddie,' said Woodhouse, nodding. 'That's the one. You remember it well. Mrs Markmaker said I should get myself to the old cleaning station outside of Modernia and I'd find someone waiting there who would tell me what to do.'

'Was it Daddy?' asked Little-Bit.

'Aye. Him and his metallic pal, here. Your father gave me a small, yellow piece of paper with a strange drawing on it and told me to head all the way up to the Green Valleys. There, he said, I'd find a narrow pathway that led to a tunnel of trees, at the end of which was a door. I was to go through the door with the note and, keeping out of sight as best I could, find a security guard with a white beard. I then had to give him the note and tell him to pass it on to Leo.'

At the mention of his name, Leo sat up a bit straighter. Woodhouse winked at him, then continued.

'This Leo chap was then to put the note inside a lunch box belonging to someone called Peanut. I had no idea what all this meant. It sounded like some sort of strange code to me. Now, of course, I know that it was referring to you lot: Gary's bairns.'

'And you did all that every single time? For all of the notes that I collected?' asked Leo, impressed that someone had worked as hard as he had on the Post-it mission.

'That I did, laddie. Kept me fit, that's for sure.' The rat grabbed his tail with both paws and started to lift it repeatedly above his head as if it were a barbell.

'Didn't anybody in the gallery ever spot you?' asked Peanut.

'Och, London is full of rats,' he replied. 'I barely got a second glance. Anyway, nobody would ever suspect a lowly creature such as myself of any wrongdoing. To be honest, most humans don't like rats and steer well clear of us.' He looked over at Rockwell, who was unable to suppress his shudder this time.

Feeling guilty, the boy got up to walk to the other end of the submarine. As he stood, he glanced towards 67. He could have sworn he saw the RAZER's eye momentarily flick from green to red.

7

The Power of the Pencil
and the Artist Who Wields It

eanut opened her eyes. It took her a few seconds to remember where she was, but when she saw Little-Bit fast asleep on one of the submarine's metal benches curled up next to a snoring rat, it all came flooding back. After Woodhouse's story, they'd barely been able to keep their eyes open and had all fallen asleep. Even 67 had powered down. Dad, meanwhile, had continued to drive the submarine through the night.

Peanut rose quietly, walked to the front of the submarine and hooked her arm through the crook of her dad's. She rested her head on his shoulder and he patted it gently like he always used to do.

'How long have we been going for?' she asked. 'My watch is broken.'

'About six hours, I think,' he said, pushing the periscope away and looking at his daughter. 'Only a few more to go. Can't sleep?'

She smiled. 'Not anymore. I'd like to, but my brain has other ideas. It has a lot to process, I guess.'

'That is true enough,' he replied. 'Well, seeing as you're here, would you like to have a go at driving?'

Dad stood up and Peanut took his place in the box seat, pulling the periscope's eyepiece towards her. To her surprise, she could see the gently rippling surface of the water, fluorescent with pinks, oranges and yellows. It was as if she were flying just above it. The colourful liquid provided a stark contrast to the cold, grey steel of the cleaning channel's walls and ceiling.

'Dad, you were going to tell me why we have to go to the Green Valleys,' said Peanut, quietly so as not to wake the others. 'I mean, why couldn't I have just drawn another door with Little Tail back in the cleaning station when we first arrived?'

'It's a great question,' said Dad, 'and one I wouldn't have been able to provide a satisfactory answer to a few months ago. But, fortunately, I can now.'

'Did you read something in one of your history books, then?'

'I did indeed. In *The Power of the Pencil and the Artist Who*

Wields It by Tobermory Sketch. Nearly two hundred years old, but reads like it was written yesterday.'

'What did it say?'

'Well, Mr Sketch believes that whenever someone is creating something – a painting, a sculpture, a print, or even just a quick doodle – they can't help but put a bit of themselves into that piece of art. That's why, he says, everybody's drawings are totally unique. You and I could sit here and draw a picture of the same apple, using exactly the same materials, but our drawings would end up looking totally different.'

'Yes, I've always thought that too,' said Peanut. 'It's one of the things I love most about art. Just by taking something that you see or feel inside, and putting it down onto canvas or paper, you are revealing a piece of your soul. Everyone is different. And there is no right or wrong answer when it comes to drawing.'

'Exactly, my little artist,' said Dad, squeezing Peanut's shoulder. 'And Mr Sketch takes this idea further. He says that the *place* where you create your art can also influence it. Which is, I guess, why it's often better to paint or draw from life than it is to copy a photo. Think about it. When you're standing in a gallery looking at Monet's painting of water lilies, you can almost *feel* that cool Normandy breeze on your face as it comes in from the Seine. You can *smell* the peonies. You can *hear* the gentle lapping of the water. Not only is there a piece of Monet himself in that painting, but there is also

a piece of the place where he painted it – his home, Giverny.'

'But what's that got to do with the Green Valleys?'

Dad looked back down the length of the submarine. Little-Bit, Rockwell and Woodhouse were still fast asleep; 67 was upright, but in energy-saving mode. Their eyes were dark.

'Peanut, did you ever wonder why the very first door you drew with Little Tail, the one in your bedroom, led you to Chroma? Did you ever ask yourself why it didn't take you somewhere else? Anywhere else? You had a whole planet's worth of possible destinations, after all.'

'I— er— Well, no,' stammered Peanut. 'I guess I haven't thought about it before.'

'Why would you?' said Dad. 'Some things just work. And when they just work, there's no need to question them. But, I think, if you were to delve a bit deeper, you'd find that it brought you to Chroma because, on some level, you *wanted* to come to Chroma. Even though you didn't know that it existed. It's where *I* was and you wanted to find *me*. That – coupled with the fact that you drew the door inside the house *I* once lived in, with the pencil *I* gave you – is the reason it took you to Chroma. It was the same deal when you drew the handle on the Post-it note door. *You* made that door lead to where I was. The power of the pencil *and* the artist who wields it. There is a connection there.'

'Hang on,' said Peanut, confused. 'Are you saying that I need to draw the door in the Green Valleys, and not somewhere else, in order for it to take us to Mum in Milan?'

'Look, I'm not certain,' admitted Dad, 'but the area of Chroma that has the most connection to Milan is the Green Valleys. That is our Renaissance district. According to the books, so many famous artists from that period have, in the past, made their temporary home in the Valleys. And don't forget, Milan is widely considered to be the birthplace of the Renaissance movement.'

'But . . . but . . . what if it doesn't work?'

'Oh, I think there is a very high chance that it will,' replied Dad, confidently. 'After all, you *really* want to find your mum, right? Just like you *really* wanted to find me?'

'Of course.'

'Then I think we have a good shot at it working. You will be drawing the door with Pencil Number One, after all. That is a pretty powerful pencil. And you, my girl, are a pretty powerful artist.'

Peanut blushed at the compliment. She pulled Little Tail from her bandolier and, as if holding it for the first time, had an even greater understanding of the pencil's power.

'Now, why don't you try to get some more sleep,' Dad said gently. 'We need you to be in full working order when we get to the Green Valleys.'

Peanut stood, let him take the seat back and turned to leave the cockpit. 'Dad,' she said.

'Yes?'

'Thank goodness for those books, eh?'

'Thank goodness, indeed,' he replied. 'You can always find the answers you need in the pages of a good book.'

Arrival

'R ise and shine, sleepyheads!'

Dad, with 67 by his side, walked back through the submarine, nudging Peanut, Little-Bit, Rockwell, Leo and Woodhouse to wake them from their slumbers.

'Welcome to the Green Valleys cleaning station,' he said. 'Now, let's get back onto dry land, shall we?'

The children lined up behind Dad as he unlocked the round hatch, then they followed him through the airlock and into the lift. 67 pressed the *up* button and, with a jolt and a judder, they headed to ground level accompanied by the now familiar hissing sound of the pressure adjuster.

'So, Mr Jones, what's the plan?' said Rockwell as they

began the long walk down the corridor towards the Green Valleys cleaning station.

'Well, first we'll grab some refreshments – we still have some time before the sun rises in Milan – then we'll head out into the Green Valleys to the spot where Peanut is going to draw our door. And then we're off to Italy!' It sounded like Dad was about to take them all on holiday.

'Hang on,' said Leo, stopping. 'What do you mean *we're* off to Italy?'

'Well, Woodhouse and 67 can't come with us, obviously,' replied Dad, mindful of the fact that illustrations made in Chroma crumble to dust as soon as they are touched by human hands in the real world. 'But the five of us should be able to handle Mr White.'

'No way,' replied Leo. 'You *can't* come with us, Dad. Last night, you claimed to be Conté's heir. You said yourself that you're one half of the Resistance's ultimate weapon against White! What was the point in staying hidden all of this time if you're then just going to walk straight up to him in broad daylight? I might be new to this world and all of its crazy rules, but even *I* can see that that's exactly what White wants you to do. Why else would he have taken Mum if not to draw you out of hiding? You *have* to stay in Chroma. It's too dangerous for you to go to Italy.'

'If you think for one second that I'm going to let the

four of you go to Milan without me, then you've got another thought coming. You can't capture that man on your own!'

'Daddy,' said Little-Bit, 'don't forget that Peanut, Rockwell and I have done pretty well by ourselves so far. And now we have Leo with us too. Even if we can't catch Mr White ourselves, I'm sure we can lure him back to Chroma. Then you, the Markmakers and the rest of the Resistance can capture him when we come through the portal.'

'Mr Jones,' said Rockwell, 'I'd be lying if I said that heading to Milan without a grown-up to confront one of the world's scariest people wasn't absolutely terrifying, but – bigger picture – there's *no* way you can be there with us. Anyway, Little-Bit's plans usually work, so I think we should trust her.'

'The humans are correct, Gary Jones,' said 67. 'You must remain in Chroma. We will travel, sub-aquatically, to the Spire via the eastbound cleaning channel and wait there for the children to return with Mr White and Tracey Jones.'

Everybody turned to look at Peanut, who had yet to say anything. The idea of leaving her father so soon after they had been reunited was awful, but deep down she knew that it was the right thing to do. He needed to be kept safe at all costs. After a moment or two, she finally spoke.

'Dad, it'll be OK. Rockwell, Leo, LB and I can get Mr White and Mum back to Chroma, I just know it. You have to trust us. We've come this far, and we won't let you down now. Remember, we also have *this* to help us.'

She lifted a shaky hand and pulled Little Tail from her bandolier. As she pulled it from its slot, it slipped from her fingers, hitting the floor with a surprisingly loud thud before rolling to a stop at Leo's feet. He bent down to pick it up, but just as his hand was about to close around the pencil, Woodhouse swooped in and grabbed it.

'Oh my,'
said the rat,
holding it with two paws.
'I've always wanted to get my
claws on Pencil Number One, ever
since Mammy first told me about
it when I was a wee pinkie. Och,
I wish she could see me now.'

Dad watched as the rat handed Little Tail back to Peanut, who carefully put it back in her bandolier.

'OK,' he said with a sigh. 'I suppose you're right. I'll stay in Chroma with Woodhouse and 67. We'll head to the control room at the top of the Spire and meet the four of you, Mr White and Mum there. Peanut, remember what I said about you being in control of where that pencil takes you. You need to *really* want to come to the Spire.'

'Don't worry, Dad. We'll be there.'

'OK, well, I think it's time we headed out to Caravaggio's Folly, then. Let's get this show on the road.'

Caravaggio's Folly

The path they followed led from the cleaning station's door and skirted the outer limits of the Green Valleys. It was very narrow and *very* overgrown. In fact, the group had to pause every few metres so that 67 could cut back the dense, tangled knots of oil-painted bramble that blocked their way. At least the brier provided some cover to help keep the group hidden.

'Peanut, these actually taste nice,' said Rockwell, munching on one of the sandwiches that Peanut had sketched for them back at the station. 'You're getting better at drawing snacks.'

'Agreed,' said Little-Bit. 'My jam sandwich

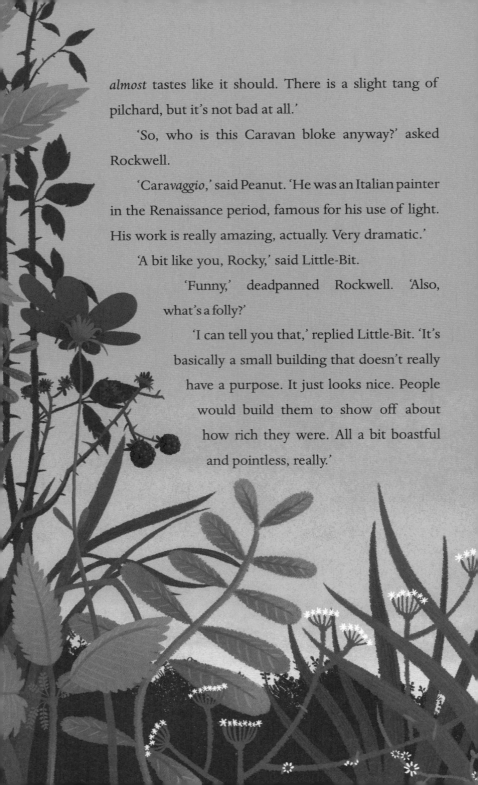

almost tastes like it should. There is a slight tang of pilchard, but it's not bad at all.'

'So, who is this Caravan bloke anyway?' asked Rockwell.

'Cara*vaggio*,' said Peanut. 'He was an Italian painter in the Renaissance period, famous for his use of light. His work is really amazing, actually. Very dramatic.'

'A bit like you, Rocky,' said Little-Bit.

'Funny,' deadpanned Rockwell. 'Also, what's a folly?'

'I can tell you that,' replied Little-Bit. 'It's basically a small building that doesn't really have a purpose. It just looks nice. People would build them to show off about how rich they were. All a bit boastful and pointless, really.'

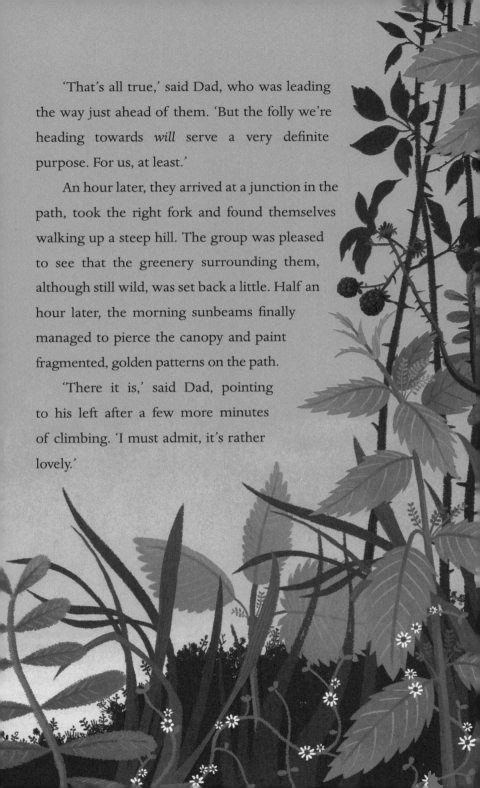

'That's all true,' said Dad, who was leading the way just ahead of them. 'But the folly we're heading towards *will* serve a very definite purpose. For us, at least.'

An hour later, they arrived at a junction in the path, took the right fork and found themselves walking up a steep hill. The group was pleased to see that the greenery surrounding them, although still wild, was set back a little. Half an hour later, the morning sunbeams finally managed to pierce the canopy and paint fragmented, golden patterns on the path.

'There it is,' said Dad, pointing to his left after a few more minutes of climbing. 'I must admit, it's rather lovely.'

Right in the centre of a picturesque meadow was a small but extraordinarily beautiful building sitting at the top of the rise, overlooking the valleys. It featured an elegant round tower, about five metres tall, with a domed roof.

Surrounding the tower was a circular balcony held up by a series of grand columns.

'Ionic,' said Little-Bit.

'Yeah. I— er— was about to say that,' said Rockwell.

'Hand-painted by Caravaggio himself during his stay in Chroma. Late sixteenth century, I believe,' added Dad. 'Such form. Such symmetry.'

'Oh look!' said Leo. 'There's some sort of bird perched on the roof. It looks a bit like a peacock. And there are two more flying above us.'

'KALEIDOSCOPPI!' shouted Peanut, Little-Bit and Rockwell in unison.

'Kaleido-what now?' said Leo.

'Shh!' said Dad. 'Remember, we don't want to draw attention to ourselves.' He looked at the gold-crested creature sitting proudly atop the folly, and the red- and green-crested creatures that circled overhead. 'They are rather beautiful though.'

The kaleidoscoppi were a near-extinct breed of bird native to Chroma whose song was believed to inspire

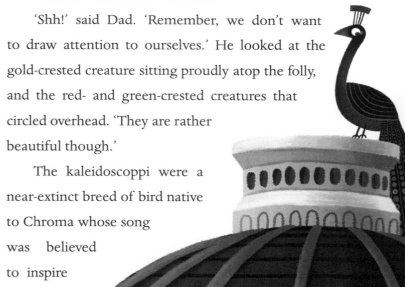

creativity in whoever heard it. Peanut, Rockwell and Little-Bit had met them a few times before, and these meetings had always lifted their hearts. Peanut suspected that their presence at the folly was to give the group a much-needed confidence boost just before they embarked on their mission in Milan. The birds had always seemed to be in the right place at the right time, after all.

'Right, let's get on with it,' said Dad. 'Woodhouse, do your thing.'

The rat was despatched to scamper across the meadow and make sure the coast was clear. When he gave them the sign, the other six ran the short distance to the folly. They found a door in the wall behind the columns and quietly entered the cool, circular room.

'Ooh, it reminds me of the catacombs in Paris,' said Rockwell, running a finger along the damp brickwork and remembering their recent adventure in the French capital.

'Let's hope that a policeman doesn't turn up and steal your other shoe,' laughed Peanut. Rockwell chuckled along with her at the memory.

'OK, Peanut,' said Dad. 'This is it. It's your time to shine.'

She took a deep breath, lifted Little Tail from her bandolier and started to draw a door. The smooth line that came from the ultra-sharp tip hung perfectly in the air. It was beautifully illuminated by the light streaming

in through the single window. The entire scene looked as though it could have been painted by Caravaggio himself.

Five minutes later, Peanut was done.

'Is that OK?' she asked Dad, her eyes shiny in anticipation of his approval.

'It's perfect,' he replied. 'I've said it before and I'll say it again: you are such a talented artist, Peanut.' He turned to face the others. 'All right, team. It's time. Be careful, and don't do anything rash. Just bring your mother and Mr White back here to Chroma. Get them to the Spire and Woodhouse, 67 and I can do the rest. Kids, keep each other safe, OK?'

The three Jones children and Rockwell all nodded firmly.

Peanut took a deep breath and reached out to grab the illustrated doorknob. It felt cold in her hand. She rotated it a quarter-turn anti-clockwise and smiled as something clicked. She looked back at her dad.

'Promise you'll be there when we get back?' she said.

'I promise,' he replied.

Then Peanut turned to the door, pushed it open and walked through, followed by Leo, Little-Bit and Rockwell. The distant song of the kaleidoscoppi provided the soundtrack to the children's journey through the dimensions.

10
The Church of
Santa Maria delle Grazie

They emerged into an empty rectangular room with high, vaulted ceilings that, to Peanut's eye, resembled bat wings. The pale walls were featureless, except for a small door on the left towards the far end and several high windows on the right.

'So, are we in Milan?' asked Leo.

'No idea,' said Rockwell. 'But we are in a church of some sort. It could be Catholic, I guess, which might suggest we're in Italy.'

'Yeah. And I can hear motorbikes zooming past outside.

Italian people love riding around on scooters, don't they?' said Little-Bit.

'Oh, we're definitely in Milan,' said Peanut, who was facing in the opposite direction to the others, staring up at the wall directly behind them. 'Look.'

Rockwell, Little-Bit and Leo turned around. The door they had just walked through was in the centre of another much wider wooden door. Immediately above that, and stretching across the full width of the room, was a painting.

It featured a long table covered in a white cloth strewn with several items of food. Behind the table was a crowd of people, all men, who looked like they were arguing. One figure, right in the centre of the picture, sat slightly apart from the others and was looking down serenely at his open left hand.

'We must be inside the church of Santa Maria delle Grazie,' said Peanut. 'That painting is *The Last Supper* by Leonardo da Vinci.'

'Whoa!' said Rockwell. 'Even *I've* heard of that one.'

'Incredible mastery of perspective,' said Little-Bit thoughtfully as she gazed up at the fresco. 'Look how he matches the lines in the background of the painting to those of the church itself. It makes this whole room seem bigger.'

'I don't understand. What do you mean?' said Leo, which prompted his youngest sister to embark on a long and detailed explanation of something called *trompe l'oeil*, or 'trick of the eye'.

While Leo and Little-Bit discussed quadrature and matte painting, Rockwell walked over to Peanut, who had headed back to the illustrated door they'd come through. She grabbed the handle and held it until the drawing began to crumble away, leaving a fine, silvery-grey powder on the floor.

'Why did you do that?' asked Rockwell.

'I don't want to give White the opportunity to get back to Chroma until we're ready to take him there ourselves. The fewer chances he has to escape, the better,' she replied.

'Ah, I see,' he said. Then he paused, bit his bottom lip and took a deep breath. 'Peanut, can I ask you a question?' he said, quietly.

'Sure,' she replied, wiping the dusty pencil remnants from her hands.

'What do you think of 67?'

'What do I think of 67?' She frowned. 'Erm, well, I'm really grateful to them for helping my dad to escape from the Spire. That's about it really. Why? What do you think of them?'

'Well, er, obviously it's great that they helped set your dad free and everything, but I can't help but think that there's something a bit . . . funny about them.'

'Funny?' said Peanut. 'What do you mean?'

'Well, they just seem kind of . . . untrustworthy,' he replied.

'Untrustworthy?' Peanut's frown deepened. 'Rockwell, is this because they called you out that one time? I understand how that would annoy you, but—'

'NO!' He cut her off. 'Well, yes. But it's not just that. A few times I've noticed . . . well, let's just say that something feels slightly off with 67.'

'Rockwell, I'm going to stop you right there,' said Peanut abruptly, holding her hand out like a stop sign. 'This robot saved my dad. End of story. They put everything at risk by betraying Mr White and the other RAZERs. In fact, I'd say that if anything feels *slightly off*, it's the fact that you can't cope with someone – or something – being smarter than you are. I think you need to get over this right now.'

'Hang on a second, I—'

He didn't get to finish his sentence because at that very moment the door at the far end of the room opened with a loud bang. All four children turned to face it just as the first of three very familiar figures walked confidently into the church.

Surprise

Nerys was the first through the door. She immediately turned to face the children and smiled.

Next came Mum. Unlike Nerys, she didn't look over to where the children were straight away. Instead, she looked upwards, taking in the church's interior.

'Ooh, it's much smaller than I imagined,' she said. 'Now, where's this painting then?' She turned to her right and saw Peanut, Little-Bit, Leo and Rockwell standing below *The Last Supper*.

She froze, mouth agape.

'K-kids?' she stammered, after a second or two. 'But . . . but . . . you're on a sleepover at the Science Museum! What

on earth are you doing *here*? In *Milan*?' She shook her head and rubbed her eyes like a cartoon character. When she realised that she wasn't dreaming and that her children were actually in the room, she ran over to give them a giant hug, pulling Rockwell in to join them too. All four children hugged her back, relieved that she was safe and that Mr Stone was nowhere to be seen.

Peanut's brain was whirring as she buried her head in the embrace. Having been caught off guard by Mum and Nerys's prompt arrival, she hadn't yet had the chance to formulate a proper plan of action.

She decided to use the hug as an opportunity to do some quick thinking. She caught Little-Bit's eye and mouthed the words 'What now?'

The younger girl frowned. It looked like she was thinking hard too.

All too soon, Mum released her grip.

And then a third figure walked into the church.

12
Stone

r Stone was dressed in his usual black suit, black shirt and black tie (with very, very, very dark grey polka dots). On his head was a dazzling white fedora, pulled down low over his brow.

He stopped and turned towards the group. His eyes narrowed, then he smiled widely, revealing a set of perfectly even, white teeth.

'Milton, did you organise this?' said Mum, grinning. 'Oh, of course you did! It's because it's Leo's eighteenth birthday tomorrow, isn't it? How KIND of you! And to think, when I mentioned it last week, you pretended to ignore me. Oh, thank you! Thank you so much. What a lovely surprise. Children, say "thank you" to Mr Stone for flying you over to Italy. Aren't we all lucky?'

Mr Stone's smile slipped slightly, and Peanut thought she could see confusion in his eyes. Or maybe it was a flash of anger. Whatever the emotion, it was only there for a split second. His teeth soon reappeared and normal, slimy service was resumed.

He turned to face the children. 'Hello, Tracey's offspring. It's delightful to see all, er, four of you,' he said, his voice positively dripping with smarm. 'Especially you, *Pernilla*. We are old friends, after all.'

A wild fury was beginning to boil in the pit of Peanut's stomach, not least because he'd called her by her hated given name, Pernilla.

'I must say,' he continued, 'what a wonderful treat it is to see you here.' He looked directly at Peanut. 'As your mother said, it's *just* as I planned.'

A shiver ran down Peanut's spine as Stone's smile widened. She grabbed her mother's hand and pulled her to one side. 'Mum, are you OK?' she whispered. 'Has he hurt you?'

'Hurt me?' asked Mum with a perplexed expression on her face. 'Seriously, Peanut, I'm starting to get a bit worried about you. Why on earth would you think Mr Stone is trying to hurt me?'

But before Peanut could answer, Nerys appeared at Mum's shoulder.

'Hello, my lovelies. So sorry to interrupt. Er, Peanut, do you think I could have a quick word with you?' She opened her eyes wide and flicked her head to one side in a *come-with-me-right-now* kind of way.

Peanut smiled at Mum, let go of her hand and followed Nerys to the far side of the room. Once there, the woman began speaking very quickly.

'I don't know how you got here so fast,' said Nerys, her voice urgent and shaky, 'but thank goodness you did. Now, I know this will sound silly, but you *have* to believe me. I think that Mr Stone . . .' she swallowed loudly, 'has taken us HOSTAGE.' She glanced anxiously over to where the man in the white fedora was standing. 'And I don't even know why! Please, *please* will you help us? I'm so scared that something awful is going to happen.'

Nerys Tells Them the Truth

Whenever Peanut and Nerys had met in the past, she had always been such a jolly, calming presence. As such, the obvious fear in her voice was even more unsettling.

'Of *course* I'll help you. But . . . but . . . when I just mentioned Mr Stone to Mum, she—'

'She made out that you were crazy for thinking that he would do anything to hurt her? I know! That's been her response to me too! I think that he must have brainwashed her or something. She's totally convinced that we're all just having a nice little city break. She didn't even flinch when he took our passports from us and said we'd be staying in Milan for a few weeks. I'm not gonna lie to you, I'm absolutely terrified.'

'So what has White, er, Stone, said to you then?' asked Peanut.

'Nothing that made any sense,' she whispered. 'Last night, after the ballet, he started to behave very strangely. When I reminded him that we were due to fly back to London straight after we'd seen *The Last Supper*, he just smiled smugly, shook his head and said something about not going anywhere until the *heir* arrives. I had no idea what he was talking about. The heir of *what*?'

That explains the flash of anger, thought Peanut. White must be cross because Dad – Conté's heir – hadn't shown up with them. Thank heavens they'd persuaded him to stay back in Chroma.

'I just wish we weren't in Milan,' continued Nerys. 'We're so far away from home. What I'd give to just . . . teleport away from this place.'

Peanut smiled and brought her hand up to Little Tail. Then she grabbed Nerys by the shoulders and looked her straight in the eye. 'Don't worry. I'm going to rescue you both, I promise. I've got a plan, but you're going to have to trust me. And you're going to have to help.'

'Of course,' said the woman. 'What do you need me to do?'

'You need to take Mum over to the painting and keep her looking at it for a few minutes. Then I want you to bring her and Mr Stone outside the church. I'll be waiting for you with Rockwell, LB and Leo, and we're going to get you out of here. Whatever happens, don't leave Stone on his own with Mum. Do you think you can do that?'

'Er, yes, I think so,' replied Nerys. 'So just a few minutes with the painting?'

'Yes,' said Peanut, reassuringly. 'That should give me enough time.'

She let go of Nerys's shoulders and walked back over to

her mother, who was lovingly redoing Little-Bit's plaits. She caught her sister's eye and winked at her. Little-Bit seemed to understand what was happening and nodded slightly in return.

'Er, Mum,' said Peanut, smiling. 'Look, I'm really sorry about that stuff I said about Mr Stone. I think I'm a bit, er, tired. It's been a busy morning already. In fact, maybe we should all wait for you outside. You know, get some fresh air while you have a look at the painting. Shall we see you in a few minutes?'

'OK, darling,' she said, handing Peanut a ten-euro note. 'And maybe get yourselves a lemonade or something too. You do look a bit frazzled.'

14
The Jerusalem Plate

Outside, Peanut got to work quickly. She was standing on a narrow pathway that ran around the outside of the church, hidden from the eyes of the tourists that were in the square. She had Little Tail in her left hand and was drawing a picture of a door on the wall as quickly as she could. As the point danced smoothly across the brickwork, she remembered what Dad had told her about the power of the pencil and the artist who wields it.

She tried her best to concentrate her thoughts on the Spire, specifically Mr White's control room at the top of it. That's where she needed this door to lead to, after all. Fortunately, it wasn't long since she had been there with Little-Bit and Rockwell, so it felt fresh in her mind.

Two minutes later, Peanut was done. She stood back and admired her work. Then she slipped the pencil into its slot on her bandolier, walked around the corner through a small gate and – into the square right outside the church.

The sight that greeted her made her heart sink.

Mr Stone was standing with a nervous-looking Leo, Little-Bit and Rockwell, talking very animatedly. Peanut rushed over.

'What do *you* want? Where's Mum?' she shouted.

'Ah, here she is,' sneered Mr Stone. 'Little *Pernilla*. Don't worry, your mother will be out in a minute. In the meantime, as I was just telling the kindergarten class here, I've got a bone to pick with you, *girl*.'

He grabbed Peanut by the arm and pulled her roughly towards him.

'If you think for one second that you're going to derail my plans, then you are sorely mistaken.' His snarling face was so close to Peanut's she could feel his hot breath on her eyeballs. 'You will NOT ruin this for me! So when *Mummy* comes out, why don't you give her one of your repulsive little hugs, tell her you have some homework to finish and then scuttle off back to whichever filthy little cave the four of you emerged fr—'

Suddenly, he stopped talking. Nerys had appeared, silently, next to the group. Stone paused for a beat, smiled and let go of Peanut's arm, tapping her affectionately on the head as he stepped backwards.

Peanut's heart was beating wildly. This man was *so* dangerous. She would *not* let him hurt Mum. Or Nerys, who returned her shocked stare with an 'I-told-you-so' look in her eye.

'YOO-HOO, EVERYONE! HERE I AM,' shouted Mum in a sing-song voice as she came out of the church door

and skipped over to the group. 'What's going on here then? Has something happened?'

'Oh no, no, no, no, no, no,' said Stone. 'I was just . . . apologising to Pernilla for the fact that the return flight I booked for them was leaving so soon. Unfortunately, it was all I could get at such short notice.'

'Return flight?' said Mum, looking down at her daughter. 'Oh. When are you leaving?'

'Any minute now, actually,' said Stone before Peanut could answer. 'Flying visit. So I suppose, sadly, that we should say our goodbyes. It has been a *delight* to see you all, though.'

Nerys subtly kicked Peanut's foot and looked at her with pleading eyes.

'Er, yes,' said Peanut. 'I'm afraid he's right. It's only a flying visit. But don't worry because before we go we've arranged for, um, a private view of, er, that, er, that other priceless artefact. You know, the really famous one that is also kept in this church.'

'Another priceless artefact? Other than *The Last Supper*?' asked Mum, perplexed.

'Exactly,' replied Peanut. 'You know, it's the . . . it's the . . .'

'It's the Jerusalem Plate!' interrupted Little-Bit. 'You know, the *actual* plate that Jesus used at the *actual* Last Supper. They keep that here as well. In fact, I think it still has a bit of Jesus's dinner on it.'

'Really?' said Mum. 'I've never heard of the Jerusalem Plate.'

'Er, no. Not many people have,' said Rockwell. 'Only a very select group of people ever get to see it.'

'That's right,' added Leo. 'Fortunately, Mr Stone here is very well-connected and has managed to get us all a pass.'

Mum turned to Nerys, who smiled and nodded her head enthusiastically.

'And the thing is,' said Peanut, looking down at her non-existent watch, 'we have to go in right now. We only have a small window of time, you see.'

'Oh. OK then,' said Mum. 'Well, again, that's so kind of you, Milton. I guess we'd better go in.'

'Yes,' Stone replied suspiciously. 'I guess we'd better go in.'

'Follow me,' said Peanut. 'The door is just around the corner.'

She led the group through the small gate and onto the narrow pathway.

'Here we are,' she said, when they got to her illustration.

She put her hand on the graphite handle and carefully turned it. The latch clicked, and she pulled the door open.

'After you,' she said politely. And then she ushered the entire party through, closing the door behind her just as it started to crumble.

15
The Darkness

'**I** can't see anything,' said Mum. 'Do they have to keep it dark in order to protect the Jerusalem Plate?'

Peanut didn't reply. She was also wondering why none of the lights were on. It was especially frustrating because she wanted to be sure that they had arrived in the right place – the room at the top of the Spire.

'This is ridiculous!' boomed Mr Stone. 'Hang on . . .'

Two seconds later, a small but brilliant white light lit up the whole place.

'That's better,' said Stone, holding his phone aloft, its torch blazing brightly.

The relief that Peanut felt when she recognised the control room soon disappeared when she realised that it was empty. Where were they? Dad, Woodhouse and 67 were supposed to be waiting there, ready to apprehend Mr White. They'd had long enough to get to the Spire, what with the time difference and everything.

Something must have happened, she thought.

'So, where is this plate then?' asked Mum.

'I was wondering the same thing,' said Nerys.

'Where, indeed?' said Stone as he walked slowly around the large console jam-packed with switches, levers and buttons.

The children looked anxiously at one other. Rockwell mouthed *What's going on?* Peanut shrugged.

Stone crouched down and pulled

hard at something on the floor. Suddenly, his face glowed with a multitude of bright rainbow colours. He had opened the trapdoor that led to the huge pool of Rainbow Lake water under the control-room floor. Stone looked up and smiled.

'Beautiful,' he said, his voice oilier than ever.

That's when it happened.

Stone moved so quickly that it didn't quite seem real. First, he flipped backwards and began to levitate, horizontally, a metre from the floor. Then he started to spin really, *really* fast. His white fedora flew from his head and landed right at Nerys's feet.

Mum gasped. 'MILTON!? Stop it! You're scaring me! Peanut, WHAT IS GOING ON!?' she yelled.

'I-I don't know,' replied Peanut. She turned to Nerys, who had picked up the hat and appeared to be quite enjoying the sight of Stone revolving rapidly.

After a few seconds, Stone's spinning slowed before eventually stopping altogether.

'I think he's got something wrapped around him,' said Rockwell, 'Hang on. Is he . . . tied up?'

Sure enough, Mr Stone was wrapped tightly in thick, jet-black rope, its coils binding him from his chest to his knees.

'AARRRRGH!' he squealed, the desperation in his high-pitched voice clear for all to hear. 'SOMEBODY, HELP ME!'

The confused expressions on the children's faces suddenly transformed into four wide grins as, slowly, a muscular female figure emerged from the shadows behind Mr Stone. Only then did it become apparent to Peanut that the man wasn't actually levitating after all; he was being held up by this woman who was dressed in a tight, black spandex suit. Billowing out behind her was a black cape emblazoned with a large, grey letter D.

Then an equally muscular male figure appeared, wearing a dark brown body stocking and a green cloak.

'Greetings, citizens!' he said. 'And greetings . . . MR WHITE! As you can now see, there is a reason why people are often afraid of . . . The Darkness!'

16
Mission Accomplished

'TABLE GUY!' shouted Little-Bit. 'It's so good to see you. And it's very nice to meet you, The Darkness. I LOVE your suit!'

The superhero holding Mr Stone looked down and nodded her appreciation to the little girl. 'Thank you,' she said in a breathy voice. 'It's very nice to meet you too.'

Suddenly, a door on the far side of the room swung open and two small figures bustled through.

'MR AND MRS MARKMAKER!' shouted Rockwell.

The elderly couple ran to Peanut, Little-Bit and Rockwell and swallowed them in a big group hug.

'You did it!' shouted Mr M. 'You managed to get Mr White back here! We can always rely on you to deliver the goods!'

Mrs M turned to face Peanut's brother. 'And you must be Leo.'

'Y-yes,' said the older boy. 'It's, er, very nice to meet you.'

'OK, will someone tell me what the HECK is going on!?'

Everyone turned to face Mum, who was standing with her hands on her hips and an expression on her rapidly reddening face that Peanut recognised only too well. Messy bedroom face, she called it.

'I'll say it again, shall I? WILL SOMEONE TELL ME WHAT IS GOING ON?'

'Er, maybe I can help,' said a voice from the far side of the room. A man with long, curly hair was standing in the doorway in front of a tall robot and a large brown rat. Slowly, he stepped out of the shadows and into the light.

'Gary?' said Mum, quietly. 'Is . . . is that you?'

Part Two

... in which Peanut gets
out of the frying pan

17
We're Not in Italy Anymore

racey Jones walked over to her husband. She stood directly in front of him and raised a hand to move the long, curly hair from in front of his eyes.

'Hello, Tracey,' he said, smiling. 'You have no idea how much I've missed you.'

He moved to hug her, but Mum stepped backwards. She looked into his eyes as her own filled with tears. After a few seconds, she spoke.

'Gary, how could you do it?' she said quietly. 'How could you leave your children? How could you leave *me*?'

'Tracey, I didn't leave . . .' Dad began to say, but she turned around and walked away.

'I'm going straight back through that door,' Mum said. 'Milton, are you coming wi—'

She stopped herself, suddenly remembering that Mr Stone was somewhat indisposed.

'Would love to, Tracey,' said the man, his voice shaking with fear, 'but, unfortunately, I can't move. These strange people have tied me up!'

Oh, that's rich, thought Peanut. *What a faker! As if White doesn't know exactly why The Darkness and Table Guy captured him.* Peanut's anger was boiling in the pit of her stomach. Mum had to know the truth, and she had to know it right now.

Mum began to walk gingerly towards Mr Stone, looking a little afraid.

'Wait . . .' said Peanut.

'For what?' asked Mum, looking back at her daughter. Her voice was suddenly sharper. 'For me to get tied up, too? Or for your dad to walk out on us a second time? I'd rather not go through that pain again, thank you very much.'

'But, Mum, Dad *didn't* leave us!' shouted Peanut. 'He was kidnapped and brought here against his will. He's been trapped here.'

'Trapped!? Oh, *poor Dad*!' yelled Mum, spinning on her heels to face her daughter. 'It must have been terrible for hm! Italy is such a hellish place, after all. And what exactly was wrong with Mexico, Gary?' She turned to her husband with fire in her eyes. 'Too much sunshine for you? Was the ocean not quite turquoise enough? Or did you just get sick of eating all those delicious enchiladas and quesadillas? Maybe you fancied a bit of spaghetti, y'know, just for a change? Oh, PLEASE! Cry me a river!'

'Mexico?' said Dad, perplexed. 'Who said anything about Mexico?'

'But, Mum,' said Little-Bit, her bottom lip trembling. 'Dad never went to Mexico. And he wasn't living in Italy. *We're* not in Italy anymore, either. We're in a place called Chroma.'

'Peanut's right, Mum,' said Leo. 'Dad didn't leave us. He *was* taken.'

'And he was taken by *that* man!' Peanut shouted, pointing an accusing finger at Mr Stone. 'Mum, you have to understand . . . he is *not* your boss, Mr Stone. He's actually called Mr White, and he's the evil mayor of Chroma!'

Peanut wasn't surprised that Stone appeared shocked. *Typical manipulative behaviour from the world's most evil man*, she thought. Mum, on the other hand, looked completely . . . Well, Peanut couldn't figure out *what* Mum's face looked like at that moment. She'd never seen an expression quite like it.

'Oh, not you two as well?' said Mum, eyeing Little-Bit and Leo. 'Honestly, why can't you three just see the truth for

what it is. W-H-I-T-E! . . . US.' She carefully enunciated
each word, leaving a gap between them for dramatic effect.
'And, Little-Bit, what do you mean we're *not* in Italy anymore?
What is . . . Chroma? And why on EARTH would you think
that Milton is . . . this Mr White person?!'

'Tracey, *please* give me a chance to explain,' said Dad,
walking across the room towards her.

'WHY SHOULD I?' she shouted, backing away from him again. 'Give me one good reason why I should give you a chance?'

'Look around you. Does any of this look normal to you?' he said. 'And look at me! I am standing here with a massive robot, a talking rat and two actual superheroes who have just tied up your boss. Don't you think that this situation is somewhat . . . unusual?'

Mum stopped for a second and surveyed the control room at the top of the Spire – not that she *knew* that's where she was. As she took in the strange surroundings, including the robot, the rat and the superheroes, her eyes landed on some familiar-looking paintings leaning against a wall. One looked a lot like a van Gogh, and she could have sworn the other was the actual *Mona Lisa*.

She also found herself looking for the non-existent Jerusalem Plate. She had yet to work out that it had been a ruse created by her daughters to get her to Chroma. But plate or no plate, there was no denying the fact that this was one unconventional museum.

'Hang on, what do you mean a *talking* rat?' she asked.

'Ah, yes. Sorry. Terribly rude of me,' said Woodhouse, walking over to her. 'Allow me to introduce myself. My name is Woodhouse. Pleased to meet you, Mrs Jones. Gary has told me a lot about you.' He offered her his paw.

Mum blanched. She didn't take the tiny paw. Instead, her mouth started opening and closing, but no sound came out. Mr Stone looked equally bewildered by the scene playing out in front of him.

'Er, I think you'd better sit down, Mum,' said Peanut. 'You look a bit pale.'

Mrs M pulled up a chair and gently guided Mum into it.

'OK, Tracey,' said Dad. 'Are you ready for me to explain?'

She nodded.

'All right. I'm going to tell you everything.'

Dad's Story

'I t all began the night before my eighteenth birthday,' said Dad. 'I remember my mother sitting me down at the dining-room table and telling me that there was something I needed to know. A family secret.'

Mum was still staring at Woodhouse, open-mouthed. The rat, slightly disconcerted by her reaction, had climbed up onto the control panel and was trying to avoid eye contact with her.

'It was all very odd,' continued Dad. 'She said that just before he died, my father had told her that we were distantly related to a famous Frenchman called Nicolas-Jacques Conté. Apparently, he was the inventor of the pencil. Not only that, but the prototype he made, the first ever pencil, had been passed down through the generations of my father's family. Now that my father was gone and I was about to turn eighteen, it was time for me to inherit it. Then she pulled out a small wooden box and opened the lid. Inside I saw . . . *that*.'

He pointed to Little Tail. Peanut pulled it from her bandolier and held it up to show Mum.

'She said it was known as Pencil Number One,' continued Dad. 'I thought it was the most beautiful thing I had ever seen. My mother said that not only was this a very famous and legendary artefact, but that my dad had told her it also held a myriad of strange and wonderful powers. She said it was far too delicate and precious to use, so I was to keep it hidden away in its special box. Er, Tracey, are you listening?'

Mum blinked several times and then jumped slightly as she woke from her talking-rat-induced trance. She turned to face her husband. 'Er, y-yes,' she said, her crossness slowly starting to return. 'You were saying something about your mum giving you a pencil. Big deal!'

'That's not all,' Dad said. 'She also told me about a hidden city. A place called Chroma.'

'Chroma?' said Mum. 'Little-Bit, didn't you just mention Chroma?'

The little girl nodded.

'Now, this is the part that is going to be hard to get your head around, Tracey, but please try to be open-minded. Chroma is a place that exists entirely in another dimension. Only a few people ever get to visit. And it is a completely *illustrated* city.'

'Illustrated?' asked Mum. 'What on earth do you mean by that?'

'The city has been created *by* artists *for* artists. Literally. Drawn and painted and sculpted and sketched. And, what's more, Chroma is the creative hub of the entire world. Every single one of the great artists throughout history has visited the city, swum in its Rainbow Lake, and, as a result, become imbued with a wonderous sense of creativity. They've

then returned to the real world and created their incredible works of art.'

The colour was beginning to return to Mum's cheeks now. 'OK. Well, you won't be surprised to hear that I have questions,' she said.

'Of course you do, but please let me finish first,' said Dad. 'I promise I'll answer everything when I'm done.'

'Go ahead,' Mum said.

'So, my mother told me that once I turned eighteen, I could visit Chroma whenever I wanted. She even told me how to get there. Apparently, there was a secret doorway at the National Portrait Gallery. A portal to the city, she said. It was years before I actually used it, mind you.'

'Really? Why didn't you go straight there?' asked Peanut. 'I would have.'

'I don't really know,' replied Dad. 'I guess I was a bit sceptical. I'm not sure I believed Gran, to be honest. It is a pretty wild story after all.'

'You can say that again,' said Mum, sarcastically.

'Instead, I put the box away and forgot all about it.'

'So when did you visit Chroma for the first time, Daddy?' asked Little-Bit.

'It was years before I thought about the illustrated city again. Just after your gran passed away, actually. When she died, everything she had told me came flooding back. I suddenly felt a huge sense of responsibility to her and my father, and to the generations of Joneses that had gone before. I felt that it was my duty to learn more about the city, about my heritage. So I decided to go to the National Portrait Gallery. I found the portal, right behind the bust of Queen Victoria, just like Gran had said, and off I went to Chroma.'

'Gary, why didn't you tell me about all this back then?' asked Mum. Her voice was still angry, but starting to soften.

'I couldn't, Tracey,' he replied. 'You see, when I got to Chroma, I realised that there was, er, a dangerous element there, and I couldn't risk getting you and the kids caught up in it.'

'A dangerous element?' said Rockwell. 'Ah. So, that's when you learned about Mr White's plan to destroy the city and rid the world of all its creativity?'

'Yes,' said Dad. 'It's also when I joined the Resistance.'

'And soon after that, you told me about Chroma,' said Leo. 'You said certain forces were at play and you were worried that something might happen to you.'

'That's right,' agreed Dad. 'During my time with the Resistance, we learned that Mr White had heard that Conté's heir – that was me, of course – had surfaced. That made *me* the number one target. I knew that being taken prisoner – or worse – was now a distinct possibility. I also knew how important it was that the pencil was kept safe. So I decided I had to tell Leo about it and give him instructions for what to do should anything happen to me.'

'Leo, you knew?' gasped Mum.

Her son blushed and nodded.

'Mum, at first I was cross about that too,' said Peanut.

'I was angry that Leo didn't tell us that Dad hadn't left us by choice. But the truth is that Leo *couldn't* say anything. It would have put us all in danger.'

'Peanut's right,' said Dad, patting his son on the shoulder. 'Leo did nothing wrong. On the contrary, he was very, very brave. In fact, I'd go as far as to say that without Leo, Mr White would already have won. The world today would already be a much darker and greyer place.'

Leo blushed again.

'So how did Mr White capture you?' asked Peanut.

'I remember it like it was yesterday,' said Dad, turning back to his wife. 'You and the kids had gone to your sister's while I stayed at home to finish that sausage dog painting, remember? It was all going well – I had pretty much nailed that tricky paw, the one holding the violin bow – when the doorbell rang. I opened the door to find this huge guy standing there.

He was about two metres tall and two metres wide, with bright orange hair and a face I won't forget in a hurry.'

'Alan!' said Peanut, Little-Bit and Rockwell simultaneously, recognising the description of Mr White's right-hand henchman who they had helped capture on their last visit to the city.

'Before I could even say "hello", this guy put his massive arms around me in a bear hug, picked me up like I was a rag doll, and carried me out to his car. He locked me in the boot! It all happened so quickly. I immediately knew what was happening, though – that he worked for Mr White. I was terrified, lying there, trapped in total darkness. Then, after ten minutes of silence, I finally heard him get into the car.'

'That ten minutes must have been when he went into our house and left the note that was meant to look like it was from you,' said Peanut, looking across to make sure Mum was taking this in.

'I guess so. We then proceeded to drive for ages. When we eventually stopped, he opened the boot, picked me up and carried me into a building that I knew very well. Despite it being dark, I could quite clearly see where we were.'

'The National Portrait Gallery?' asked Leo.

'Yes,' said Dad. 'And it was already closed for the evening. That big bloke carried me through the empty galleries towards the bust of Queen Victoria, and we went through the portal.

We were greeted in Chroma by a platoon of RAZERs – Tracey, that is what White's evil robots are called – and I was taken straight to the Spire and put in a cell at the very top. Close to where we are right now, in fact. And there I remained, locked up, until 67 and Woodhouse rescued me.'

He turned to face his wife.

'So you see, Tracey, I *didn't* leave you,' he said. 'I was taken. And I had no way of telling you. Please know that I would NEVER leave you.'

'It's true,' said Peanut. 'You can see that now, surely.'

'They're right, Mum,' agreed Leo. 'You must admit that Dad abandoning us was pretty out of character for him.'

'Please, Mummy,' said Little-Bit. 'I can see he's telling the truth just by looking in his eyes. Can't you?'

Mum looked at Dad for a long time. Eventually, her frown began to lift and she reached out for his hand. Peanut smiled.

'OK, call me crazy, but I believe you, Gary,' she said. 'Just promise me one thing.'

'That I'll never keep secrets from you again?'

'No,' said Mum. 'That you'll get a haircut and shave off that beard.'

19
Incarcerated

'Peanut, are you absolutely sure that Milton and this Mr White are one and the same?' asked Mum, still looking bewildered as they followed the group marching Mr Stone towards the prison cells. 'And that *he* is responsible for capturing your dad?'

'Yes, Mum,' said Peanut. 'We're sure. When Dad was working for the Resistance, he'd managed to find out that White worked in your building. Plus, Stone looks exactly like White! And look at the hat!' Nerys had returned the white fedora by this point, and it was carelessly perched on Stone's head at a slightly inelegant angle. 'Also, he KIDNAPPED you, remember!? In Milan?'

'Firstly,' replied Mum, 'I'm not a kid, so how could Milton

kidnap me? And, secondly, if he *did* kidnap me, I had no idea that I had been kidnapped. Do kidnappers usually take people to the ballet after a fancy dinner at Trattoria Madonnina? I mean, we had the *tasting* menu and everything!'

'Stone is White, Mum. Trust me.'

Tracey looked over at Nerys, who nodded.

'I just find it hard to believe. *My* boss? Responsible for capturing and imprisoning *my* husband? And also masterminding a plan to rid the entire world of its creativity? It just seems so . . . unlikely. I guess I never had him down as the megalomaniacal dictator type. Although, come to think of it, he is a bit fussy about his tea. If it isn't exactly the same colour as a manila envelope, he has been known to flounce out of the room and pour it down the sink.'

'Well, the important thing is that we have him in custody now,' said Dad. 'Mr White will not be able to utilise his power anymore, Chroma can be restored to its former, technicolour glory and our family is back together again. I've missed out on too much of your lives. You are going to have to fill me in on everything that's happened while I've been locked up.'

The group arrived at the end of the corridor. Table Guy and The Darkness, on either side of the tied-up Mr White, stood with their prisoner in front of two cell doors. 67 moved forward from their position at the back of the group, banging forcefully into Rockwell's shoulder as they passed, and unlocked the door on the left. The boy scowled and the robot's eyes flashed red at him – this time Rockwell was sure of it.

'Welcome to your little hotel room, Mr White!' said Table Guy. 'I do hope you enjoy your very lengthy stay with us! Actually, that's not true! I hope you have a miserable time! You've certainly earned it!'

Mr Stone looked over his shoulder as the spandex-clad superhero pushed him into the small room on the left.

'Tracey, Nerys – please help me!' he pleaded through the tiny window once the cell door was closed. 'Tell them who I am!'

Ignoring Mr Stone's pleas and overcome by curiosity, Nerys walked over to the cell door on the right and peered through the window. Inside, sitting on the bench, was a rather tired-looking Alan. He looked up. When he saw the woman, he smiled.

'Well, hello there,' Alan said. 'Always nice to see . . . a new face.'

Nerys, spooked, jumped backward and shuffled over to stand with the others again. They all heard Alan laughing through the thick walls.

'Don't know what you're so happy about,' Mrs M shouted to Alan. 'Unless it's the fact that your new neighbour is an

old friend. That's right, we've got him, Alan! We have caught Mr White!'

Inside the cell, Alan's smile remained. He shook his head, looked down and muttered something about magic tricks. The whole exchange made Peanut feel slightly uneasy.

That uneasy feeling soon disappeared, however, when Mr M said that they should head back to the control room to meet up with Jonathan Higginbottom, Josephine Engelberger and some of the other key members of the Resistance.

'I've told them to join us immediately. There's not a moment to lose,' Mr M said. 'We have got the mother of all celebrations to plan, after all! Now that White is locked up for good, it's time for Chroma to PARTY!'

20
The Killjoy

'Yes! A ceremonial refilling of the Rainbow Lake is a BRILLIANT idea,' said Mrs M to her husband. They were among a group of giddy Resistance operatives standing beneath the portal doors that Mr White had drawn on the walls of the control room. 'And every single one of us should be there to watch. This has been a long time coming and so many good and brave people have played their part. They all deserve to be included in the celebrations.'

'Right. Decision made,' said a smiling Mr M. 'We'll do it tomorrow morning. This city has lost enough time to Mr White's regime, so let's not waste any more. Josephine, can you please work out the best way of getting the rainbow water that's up here back down to the lake? We also need to get the cleaning channels fully operational again.'

Josephine nodded.

While the Markmakers, Gary, Tracey, Leo, Nerys, 67, Woodhouse and Josephine continued to discuss the logistics of this huge and very exciting celebration, Little-Bit sat on Jonathan Higginbottom's back, both of them giggling and catching up on lost time. Doodle, the scribble-of-a-dog keen to join in the fun, kept trying to run up the alligator's tail, only to be playfully flicked off before he could reach the little girl. Peanut, meanwhile, was in the corner by herself,

looking at all the priceless paintings that Mr White had stolen. Rockwell, spotting that she was on her own, decided that this might be a good time to have an important chat with his friend. He sidled up to her.

'Er, could I have a quick word?' he asked, standing with Peanut in front of the *Mona Lisa*.

'What's up?' she asked. 'Are you thinking about how best to return these paintings to the various galleries too? I reckon we do it one at a time using White's portals, probably under cover of darkness. Best if the wider world doesn't know about Chroma. This city really should remain as secret as possible.'

'Erm, it's not that, actually,' said Rockwell as he took a deep breath. He wondered why he was so nervous about saying what he was about to say. 'I wanted to talk to you again about 67. Earlier, I . . . well . . . I saw their eyes flash red. It was weird. Look, I know you don't want to hear this, but I'm still worried that all is not quite as it seems with them and I had to tell you. I can't put my finger on what it is exactly, but my instincts are telling me that something's not right. I just don't think they're totally on our side. I really think we should confront them about it, even if it's just to prove me wrong. And if it turns that I *am* wrong, then I will apologise and won't say anything about it ever again. I promise.'

Peanut stared at Rockwell for a long moment before speaking. 'Seriously, Rockwell?' she said with more than just annoyance in her voice. 'You choose *this moment* to bring that up again!? We've just captured Mr White, we're planning to refill the lake and celebrate with the best party we've ever been to, and all you can think about is how 67 insulted you? Why do you have to be such a killjoy? Honestly, I don't know what to say.'

'No, no, no. It's nothing to do with 67 insulting me,' he replied. 'Look, I know that sometimes my mouth gets ahead of my brain, but this time I *know* that I am right. I can't explain how, but I just do. I really think you need to listen to me, Peanut. I've got this terrible feeling that if we don't do something about 67 now, we're going to regret it.'

'I'll tell you what I *am* beginning to regret,' said Peanut, her voice getting louder. 'I'm beginning to regret showing you Pencil Number One in the first place! You didn't believe me when I first told you about it, and despite everything we've been through, nothing's really changed, has it? You're still a sceptic. Why can't you just accept that sometimes people, and robots, might just decide to do the right thing? And *so what* if 67 insulted your intelligence? To be honest, at this moment in time I'm starting to think that they might have had a point!'

'Now you're just being mean,' said Rockwell, unable to disguise the hurt in his voice. 'I might not know about art and stuff like you, but I still have *feelings*.'

'Ah,' said Peanut, smirking. 'Finally, we get to the bottom

of it. You're still going on about the whole art versus science thing, aren't you? I thought we'd gotten past this. I mean, for goodness' sake, Rockwell! We are literally standing right next to a painting by Leonardo da Vinci, a guy who embodied the idea that art and science can co-exist! He proved, beyond a shadow of a doubt, that they work best when they work together. That they're dependent on each other! There is no competition to see which is best!'

'I'M NOT SAYING THERE IS, PEANUT!' yelled Rockwell, surprising himself. 'I AM JUST TRYING TO TELL YOU THAT I'M WORRIED ABOUT SOMETHING AND YOU ARE NOT LISTENING TO ME! THAT IS WHAT IS HAPPENING HERE!'

The silence that followed was the most silent silence ever. Everyone in the room had stopped what they were doing and were now looking at the two friends. They were all shocked to hear Rockwell shouting so loudly, no one more so than Peanut.

'Er, guys!' said Little-Bit, rushing over to them. 'What's going on? Why are you fighting?'

'ASK HIM!' said Peanut.

'ASK HER!' said Rockwell.

'Well, whatever's happened, I think you should both just make up. That's what Miss Gibeon tells Marley and me to do when we've had an argument at school. And today is not a day for arguments,' said the little girl, in a voice that belied her age. 'We have got lots to celebrate.'

'My point exactly!' said Peanut, folding her arms. 'I'm just not sure Rockwell is capable of having fun at the moment.' She looked at him pointedly.

'Listen, I'm sorry for shouting,' he said. 'Maybe you're right, Peanut. Maybe I'm just not in the mood for a party.' He turned his face to the wall, trying to hide the tears pricking his eyes. 'Actually, I, er, don't feel that great. So, I think I might just . . . head home. Mum is probably wondering where I am anyway.'

'I think that's a *very* good idea,' said Peanut. 'No one wants a killjoy moping about the place, sucking the fun from the celebration. I'll draw you a door, shall I? And then we can both forget that any of this ever happened.'

21
A Parting of Ways

Peanut put the finishing touches to the door handle, stepped back and returned Little Tail to its slot on her bandolier. Rockwell had suggested moving to a nearby storeroom so that he could make a quiet exit. He didn't want the fact that he was leaving to dampen the festivities, so only Little-Bit and Doodle had gone with them.

'Right, then. I guess this is goodbye,' said Peanut, coolly.

'I guess it is,' said Rockwell. He took a deep breath. 'Listen, Peanut—'

'Don't,' interrupted the girl. She didn't want to hear any emotional speeches. 'Look, maybe we were only ever meant to be study buddies, not *real* friends. I do really appreciate the help you've given me over the last few months, but, honestly, I think this is probably for the best. Now that Dad is back, my life is, hopefully, going to return to normal. I'll probably go back to Melody High, so I don't need—'

'You don't need *me* anymore,' said Rockwell, nodding.

Peanut blushed, but didn't correct him. Instead, she turned and walked away from the door she had drawn for him. 'Safe travels, Rockwell,' she said. 'Come on, LB. We've got a lot to do before tomorrow. Hurry up and say goodbye.'

Rockwell sighed, turned to Little-Bit and crouched down. She threw her arms around his neck. 'I'll see you when we get back home, Rocky. I *wish* you were staying here with us for the party, though. You are quite annoying, but it won't be the same without you.'

He hugged her back. 'I'll see you soon, LB. Have fun and keep an eye on things for me.' Rockwell then turned to Doodle and ruffled the charcoal fur around his neck. 'Goodbye, boy. I'm not sure when I'll see you again,' he said, sadly.

The dog barked three times, each woof laced with a slight whimper, and then licked Rockwell's face enthusiastically.

Rockwell stood up and wiped his cheeks. He looked directly at Peanut, but she didn't return his gaze. 'Right, I'll be off then. Say goodbye to the others for me and, well, look after yourselves.'

illustrated door and walked through, pulling it shut behind him.

Despite her anger, Peanut couldn't help but feel sad as she watched Rockwell leave. Yes, she was annoyed with him, but she was still going to miss his companionship. What really made the tears well in her eyes, however, was the fact that, deep down, she knew that he wouldn't ever be coming back to Chroma again.

22

67 and the Machines

Peanut, Little-Bit and Doodle made their way back into the control room to find everybody grouped around the console. They were still discussing plans for refilling the Rainbow Lake and the subsequent afterparty, talking loudly and with great excitement.

Peanut noticed that 67 was hovering by the trapdoor in the floor, separate from the rest of the group. They were staring into the pool of rainbow-coloured water that Mr White had been keeping there. Ironically, it was only now that Rockwell had left Chroma that a slight feeling of doubt had tiptoed its way into her mind.

What if Rockwell was right? she thought. *What if there IS something up with 67? And why am I only considering this now, rather than when Rockwell was still here?* She decided to do a bit of investigating, just to put her mind at ease.

'Hi, 67,' she said, cheerily, as she approached the RAZER.

'Hello, Medium-sized Human,' they replied in their distinctive tinny voice. 'Is there something I can assist you with?'

'Oh, nothing important,' replied Peanut. 'I was just wondering what everyone was talking about.'

The robot's eye panel rotated smoothly to their right to look at the merry group. 'The operatives still appear to be discussing party food. They have already, in my opinion, spent a disproportionate amount of time debating the merits of the French Fancy over those of the Bakewell Slice.'

'Ah, so they're tackling the important stuff,' said Peanut, nodding. 'And what have *you* been tasked with doing for the party?'

'I have not been tasked with doing anything,' replied the robot. 'But I did make a suggestion that will require some work on my part. I believe it is a good idea, and the Markmakers and the other Resistance operatives concur. So I will be actioning that presently.'

'Oh? What did you suggest?' asked Peanut.

'That we should mobilise the RAZER army to help us quicken the progress of Chroma's rehabilitation.'

'Er, what does that mean?' said Peanut, confused. 'We

should get the RAZERs to work for us?'

'Affirmative,' replied 67. 'It is a logical decision. We have a large number of very powerful and very skilled robots lying dormant in platoons all over the city. Meanwhile, we, the citizens of Chroma, have a huge rebuilding task on our hands. So why not use the very things that helped *destroy* the city to help *mend* the city?'

'That's so smart,' said Peanut. She could feel the doubt and suspicion she felt earlier tiptoeing back out of her mind.

'Your praise is appreciated, Medium-sized Human,' said the robot, curtly. 'But the fact

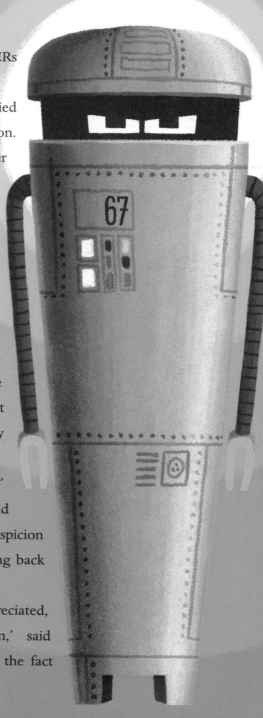

is that, as a RAZER myself, I am easily able to plug into the Spire's mainframe computer and recalibrate the directive. It's a built-in function of the second-generation RAZER model. Once docked, it's simply a question of re-engineering the core code, compiling a new binary file and distributing it using a form of high-speed transaction processing. I can apply the same method to overwrite the Big X and Exocetia programming too.'

'Wow,' said Peanut. 'So you would be in control of Mr White's *entire* army?'

'Affirmative.'

'That's amazing,' said Peanut. 'You could do so much good with all that power. Thanks so much, 67. Chroma is already in your debt, and it sounds like that debt is about to get bigger!'

'No thanks are necessary, Medium-sized Human. It's the least I can do. I want to make amends for the damage that my robotic counterparts have done to this city. Now, if you'll excuse me, I need to decrypt the security tokens and obtain authentication to the central control network.'

Satisfied that all was OK with 67, Peanut walked over to her parents and Nerys, who were discussing sandwich preferences with Jonathan Higginbottom.

'. . . Yes, yes, I totally agree, Mr Higginbottom. Triangular ones *do* taste better,' said Mum, excitedly. 'Oh, hi, Peanut.

You'll never guess what. This animated alligator cartoon character chap can TALK! Just like the rat! And, let me tell you, he *really* knows his sandwiches!'

'Hi, Mum,' Peanut said, stifling a yawn and placing her head affectionately on the alligator's shoulder. 'Yes, Jonathan Higginbottom and I are old friends.'

'You look tired,' said Dad. 'All three of you do, actually.' Leo and Little-Bit were sitting up on the control panel, eyes half-closed. 'In fact, I think that we should all get some rest. Tomorrow is going to be a big day. We have lots of things that need celebrating, not least your birthday, Leo.'

'Oh yeah, I'd forgotten about that,' he replied.

'Me too,' said Little-Bit. 'I haven't even got you a card!'

'Don't worry, LB. You can always draw one for me,' said Leo, smiling. 'I'm sure Peanut can lend you a pencil.'

23
The Big Day

The early-morning light came streaming in through the barred window of the room where the girls had been sleeping. Peanut opened her eyes and was greeted with a close-up view of Little-Bit's smiling face about three centimetres away from her own.

'At last!' giggled Little-Bit. 'I thought you'd never wake up, sleepyhead!'

Five minutes later, the sisters were dressed and standing in the corridor knocking on their brother's door.

Leo answered, bleary eyed.

'HAPPY BIRTHDAY, BIG BROTHER!' shouted Peanut and Little-Bit, before shoving eighteen giant hand-drawn balloons into his room.

'Thanks, girls. You, er, shouldn't have,' he said, stumbling backwards as he attempted to catch the balloons.

'I also painted this for you,' said Peanut, handing him a beautiful watercolour cake.

'Aw, Top-knot, this is amazing. It looks delicious!' said a delighted Leo.

'Well, looks can be deceiving. You haven't tasted it yet,' she replied sheepishly.

'HAPPY BIRTHDAY, LEO!' sang two more voices in unison, as the children's parents followed the girls into the room.

'Awww, I can't believe my little boy is eighteen!' said Mum. 'Feels like it was only yesterday that I was changing your nappies.'

'Yeah, and it must be at least a week since you stopped doing that!' Peanut said, laughing.

Leo grabbed his sister in a playful headlock and ruffled her hair.

'Ooh, Dad. Nice haircut!' said Little-Bit.

'Yes,' said Mum. 'I gave him a little trim this morning. Couldn't help myself. Made him shave too. Nice to be able to see his face again. And what a lovely face it is.'

She then gave him a huge kiss, full on the lips, much to the children's embarrassment.

'Ewww, gross!' squealed Little-Bit.

'Ugh, get a room, guys,' said Peanut, blushing.

Leo turned his head the other way. 'So, I guess you two have made up?' he asked through gritted teeth.

Dad laughed and wiped away Mum's lipstick. 'Sorry, kids. It's just that, y'know, we haven't seen each other for a long time. Anyway, many happy returns, Leo. I'm so proud of you, young man.'

Mum began cutting the painted birthday cake into slices and placing them on the pastel-drawn plates that Peanut had brought in. 'Where's Rockwell then? Still asleep?' she asked.

'No. He, er, had to head home actually,' said Peanut. 'I think he needed to see his mum.'

'Yes, of course.' Mum nodded. 'I'm sure she's been wondering where he's been. Shame he's going to miss the party, though.'

Peanut and Little-Bit shared the briefest of glances just as Mr Markmaker and Doodle appeared at the door.

'Morning, everybody,' Mr M bellowed, cheerily, as the dog ran in and jumped onto Leo's bed. 'And huge felicitations to you, Leonardo. Ooh, is that cake?' He grabbed a slice and took a big bite. '*Mmmm*, interesting flavour. You wouldn't necessarily think that liver and onions could work in this context, and yet here we are.' He put the remainder of the cake down and wiped the corners of his mouth. 'So, are we all ready to head down to the lake? The citizens are already starting to gather and it's all getting rather jolly. Millicent is holding the lift for us.'

'Oh, I think we can do better than the lift,' said Peanut, pointing to her bandolier of art supplies. 'After all, a special ceremony like this deserves a special entrance.'

24
Shallow Water

Peanut was the last to land, her descent having taken longer because of the skywriting. Once safely on the ground, she looked up and was pleased to see that she'd left the words 'I ❤ CHROMA' hanging elegantly in the air behind her. It felt like an appropriately arty contribution to the festivities.

Peanut removed her illustrated harness and started to gather up her ink-rolled wing. Once done, she took a moment to take in the scene that was unfolding around her. The Resistance operatives, many of whom she had fought beside, were buzzing with excitement and getting ready for the celebrations. But what really blew her mind was the physical transformation of the area that had taken place since she'd last stood on this spot.

It was truly remarkable. The entire crayon fence, whitewashed all those years ago on the orders of Mr White, had been restored to its former glory. It was now resplendent in reds, yellows, oranges, pinks, greens, purples and blues. The watchtowers that housed the RAZER guards had all been removed (except for one that was rigged with an enormous sound system made up of several very large speakers) and a huge opening had been cut into the fence between two of the drawbridges opposite Die Brücke – one of the city's most picturesque districts. This opening somehow made the fence feel less like a security barrier and more like a picture frame, put there to complement the dazzling view. The drawbridges on either side of the opening had been lowered to cross the lake and were already lined with crowds of cheering citizens and Resistance operatives, all eager for the refilling ceremony to begin.

And then there was the breathtaking sight of the Spire itself. From Peanut's vantage point, it looked like the tower had exploded from the ground, blasting straight into the sky before shooting out of the earth's atmosphere and into the far reaches of space. It seemed to go on forever. But, having just jumped out of an opening she'd made in a wall in the Spire a few hundred metres above where she stood now, Peanut knew that there was a pointed tippy-top up there somewhere.

The tower was still mostly white, but it wore with style the splatters of colour sustained during The Battle for The Spire. She couldn't help but wonder how magnificent it must have looked when it was first built. The smatterings of paint were likely nothing compared to its original kaleidoscopic splendour.

Peanut walked towards the opening in the crayon fence to join the others at the water's edge.

'Darling, paragliding was AMAZING!' said Mum when she saw her eldest daughter. Her face was flushed with both adrenaline and happiness. 'I never thought I'd be able to do something like that!'

'It really was fun!' said Leo. 'Thanks, Peanut. This is already shaping up to be the best birthday ever.'

Little-Bit, meanwhile, was standing at the water's edge next to Mrs Markmaker and a bemused-looking Nerys. 'I can't believe it,' the little girl said, loudly. 'Where has the water all gone? It was at least three-quarters full when we last saw it. Now it's virtually empty!'

'Well, as you know, White redirected some of it up to the pool at the top of the Spire,' said Mrs M. 'But it turns out that most of the water has been stagnating in the disused cleaning channels underneath the city. Don't worry, though. With some guidance from your father, people have been working through the night to get the channels fully operational again.

I've just been told that the water is already approaching 80 per cent effectiveness and will definitely be ready for the refilling ceremony.'

'Well, that's great news, Mrs—' Suddenly, Little-Bit stopped talking. She lifted her hand to shield her eyes from the sunlight and stared out over the lake. 'Peanut,' she said quietly. 'Can you see that? Over there.'

She pointed towards something silver and shiny lying on the lake's bed, near the opposite bank.

'I can. Hang on . . . is that . . . ?' Peanut gasped.

'Yes,' said Little-Bit, sadly. 'I think it's 72.'

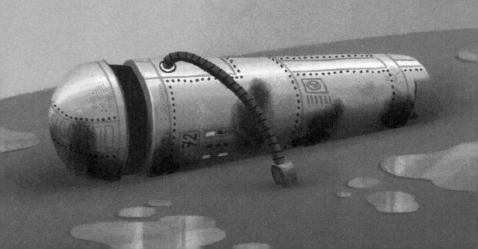

25
One Who Fell

T hat's right where it happened,' said Little-Bit, her eyes filling up. 'That's where 72 sacrificed themselves to help us.' She turned to hug Mum, unable to stop the tears tumbling down her cheeks.

Josephine Engelberger, who was standing nearby, walked over to Peanut.

'Sorry to intrude, but did I hear you say that you think that might be the RAZER who helped you first get to the Spire?' she asked.

'Yes,' replied Peanut. 'That's 72. A proper Resistance hero. And to think, they've just been lying there at the bottom of the Rainbow Lake all this time. They really should have got a proper send-off and been honoured by the city in some way. A special funeral, maybe.'

'I totally agree. They were a truly remarkable machine, by the sound of it,' said Josephine thoughtfully. 'I wonder . . .'

'You wonder what?' asked Peanut.

'Oh, er, nothing,' said the woman. 'But . . . but, yes. I think you're right, 72 should definitely get a proper send-off. I, er, I won't be long.'

Josephine walked around the edge of the lake towards the drawbridge. She stopped on the way to talk to a couple of the RAZERs who were helping to marshal the crowds – one of their first directives from 67, their new boss. After a brief conversation, the three of them continued to the drawbridge together.

When they got to the other side of the lake, they turned left and walked to the point on the bank directly above 72. The two robots then floated down towards the lifeless, horizontal RAZER, picked them up and lifted them out. Once back on the bank with Josephine, all four figures went, in a solemn procession, across the bridge and through the opening in the crayon fence, before disappearing into a door at the bottom of the Spire.

'What do you think she's going to do, Rockwell?' asked Peanut, forgetting that her friend wasn't with her in Chroma anymore. When she didn't get an answer, she felt a fresh pang of sadness.

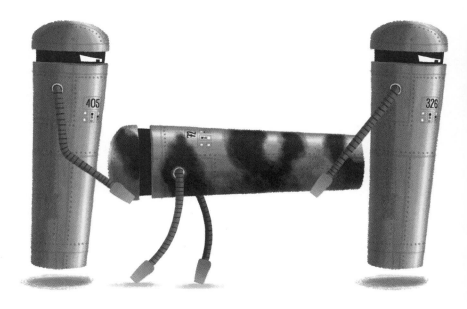

26
The Speech

The crowds around the lake had really started to amass. So had the decorations. The sky was full of balloons and kites, and hundreds of citizens held colourful banners proclaiming their love of Chroma. Folks from all twelve districts had made the journey to the centre of the city to witness this historic moment – the refilling of the Rainbow Lake. This restoration of colour and creativity was, everyone agreed, the perfect way to mark the end of Mr White's tyrannical reign.

A vast number of RAZERs, now under the supervision of 67, were lined up behind the cheering crowd on all four sides, forming a robotic border around the festivities. Some people still eyed the machines suspiciously, but most were beginning to get used to their new role, which was, they'd been told, to keep the citizens of Chroma safe.

For some reason, the sight of the RAZERs reminded Peanut of the changing of the guard at Buckingham Palace, which she'd been to watch when she was little. She supposed that the robots were destined to fulfil a ceremonial role from now on, just like those guards. This made sense because, whether people liked it or not, the RAZERs were now a part of Chroma's history.

Anyway, Peanut rather liked the way that they were being repurposed as a force for good. Even the enormous Big Xs were playing a part in the revelry. All twelve were lined up on the far bank, again just behind the crowds. Mr White had once used them in his plan to mono Chroma, but now one of them had even been painted in bright rainbow colours.

Suddenly, a microphone crackled into life, and a voice very familiar to Peanut began to boom out of the huge speakers.

'CITIZENS OF CHROMA,' said Mrs M, who was standing with her husband and Doodle on a raised platform on the far side of the lake, 'TODAY IS THE DAY.'

Her opening line was greeted by deafening cheers, which drew from her a warm smile that lit up the huge screens broadcasting the speech.

'WE HAVE SPENT MANY, MANY YEARS,' she continued, 'DREAMING OF A TIME WHEN THE

ILLUSTRATED CITY – OUR CITY – WILL BE RETURNED TO US. MY FRIENDS, TODAY IS THAT DAY.'

Peanut smiled. Who knew that Mrs M was such a great public speaker?

'OUR INKWELLS RAN DRY, OUR PAINTBRUSHES STIFFENED, AND OUR PENCILS WERE BLUNTED, BUT WE HELD ON TO HOPE AND TRUSTED THAT ONE DAY OUR PALETTES WOULD BE WET WITH COLOUR ONCE AGAIN. MY FRIENDS, TODAY IS THAT DAY.'

More cheers.

'THEY WHITEWASHED OUR WALLS, THEY MONO-ED OUR MEADOWS, AND THEY LOWERED OUR LAKE. BUT ONE THING THAT MR WHITE AND HIS CRONIES HAVE NEVER BEEN ABLE TO DO IS ERASE THE RAINBOWS THAT LIT UP OUR HEARTS THEN, AND CONTINUE TO LIGHT UP OUR HEARTS NOW.'

Even louder cheers.

'WE KNEW THAT A DAY OF RECKONING WOULD COME FOR WHITE. AND, MY FRIENDS, TODAY IS THAT DAY!'

The cheers from the crowds now were so loud that Peanut picked up Little Tail and quickly drew herself and Little-Bit some ear defenders.

Once the noise began to die down, Mrs M continued.

'WE, THE RESISTANCE, FELT IT WAS VERY IMPORTANT THAT THE PERPETRATORS OF THESE HEINOUS ACTS AGAINST US, AGAINST CHROMA, AND AGAINST ALL CREATIVITY, SHOULD BE HERE TO BEAR WITNESS TO THEIR FAILURE. WE WANT THEM TO SEE IT WITH THEIR OWN EYES.'

She gestured to her left.

'PLEASE BRING THE PRISONERS FORWARD.'

From behind the platform, Mr Stone and Alan were led to the edge of the lake by two RAZERs. Their hands were tied behind their backs. Stone, still wearing the fedora and black suit, looked confused and terrified. Alan, on the other hand, looked very relaxed. In fact, Peanut thought she saw him smiling.

'What *is it* with that guy?' she said under her breath.

'MR WHITE AND ALAN,' said Mrs M over the speakers, 'WE HAVE BROUGHT YOU HERE TO SHOW YOU THAT, DESPITE YOUR EFFORTS, CREATIVITY CAN NEVER BE DESTROYED. YOU CAN'T KEEP ART DOWN. IT WILL ALWAYS RISE TO THE SURFACE. AND YOU WILL HAVE PLENTY OF TIME TO THINK ABOUT THAT WHILE YOU SPEND THE REST OF YOUR DAYS IN PRISON. IN FACT, MAYBE YOU SHOULD TAKE UP PAINTING. IT MIGHT HELP TO PASS THE TIME.'

The crowd went even more wild. The atmosphere was electric.

'AND NOW CITIZENS OF CHROMA, FOR THE MOMENT YOU'VE ALL BEEN WAITING FOR . . .' She turned to her husband, who looked to 67 before nodding.

'. . . IT'S TIME TO LET THE WATER FLOW!'

Mrs M held up a small remote control and theatrically pressed one of its buttons. Water of all different hues started to pour out of spouts in the Rainbow Lake's wall, and it began to fill up. As the surface of the water rose, the crowd started to chant the same word in unison, over and over.

'CHROMA! CHROMA! CHROMA!'

27
From Green to Red

'I wish Rockwell were here to see this,' said Little-Bit as the rising surface of the multicoloured water twinkled in the morning sun. 'He would have loved it.'

'I know,' replied Peanut, sadly. 'I wish he were here too. He did so much to get us to this point, he really deserves to be witnessing this moment.'

She turned around to look behind her, half hoping to see Rockwell somewhere in the crowd. Instead, she saw a large group of very sweet cartoon animals, obviously visiting from the Cute Quarter. They were all holding cameras high in the air and desperately trying to take photographs of the marvellous scene playing out in front of them. A large-eyed, patterned

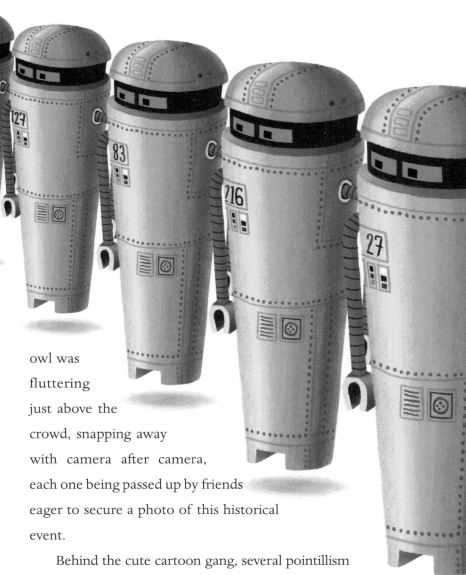

owl was
fluttering
just above the
crowd, snapping away
with camera after camera,
each one being passed up by friends
eager to secure a photo of this historical
event.

Behind the cute cartoon gang, several pointillism women wearing elegant bonnets were holding hands with men wearing towering top hats. They swayed in rhythm as they chanted along with the crowd.

Right at the back was the impressive row of RAZERs, lined

up shoulder to shoulder and floating just above the ground. They were all identical except for their numbers, and each one was staring forward blankly, their eyes glowing bright green.

Peanut let her gaze drift over to a class of rowdy comic-book schoolchildren. She was trying to read what was written in the voice bubbles above their heads, when something else caught her attention. The RAZERs' eyes all began switching from bright green to bright red, one after the other, in a kind of domino effect. Peanut followed this red wave as it made its way around the entire line of robots.

'Er, Little-Bit, look!' she shouted, struggling to make herself heard above the noise. She pulled off both her and her sister's ear defenders. 'LB! The RAZERs! Their eyes have all just changed from green to red!'

'So what?' replied Little-Bit. She was rather preoccupied with watching a ridiculously cute cartoon bushbaby trying to climb onto a cartoon red panda's shoulders.

'Didn't Rockwell say that's what happened with 67?' said Peanut. 'He told us their eyes flashed red. And, come to think of it, do you remember what happened when we were on Die Brücke with 72 that time? With all those RAZERs in the lookout towers? Their eyes went from green to red whenever we passed. Since then, I've always associated red RAZER eyes with bad news. I guess Rockwell did too! That's what he was trying to tell me!'

'Don't worry, Peanut,' said Little-Bit. '67 is in charge of the RAZERs now. I'm sure everything will be fine.'

'It just seems a bit odd, that's all. Their eyes have been green up until now.'

Peanut looked back at the line of red-eyed robots. Suddenly, and almost as if on cue, they began to move forward as one, with perfect synchronicity. Within a few seconds, they were bumping into the backs of the women in the bonnets and the men in the top hats. They, in turn, were forced to move forward and bump into the cute cartoon animals. The animals then bumped into Peanut, Little-Bit and the Resistance operatives around them. Before long, everybody in the crowd was being forced forward by the red-eyed RAZERs.

'Uh-oh,' said Peanut as she shuffled towards the edge of the lake. 'I've got a bad feeling about this. I'm starting to think that I should have listened to Rockwell!'

28
Caged

It didn't take long for the crowd to start panicking. The natural reaction was to push back against the slowly advancing RAZERs, but it soon became obvious how fruitless that endeavour was. The huge robots just kept moving relentlessly forward.

The first citizens to fall into the Rainbow Lake were those who had been standing on the drawbridges to Peanut's right and left. There were a few single fallers at first, each splash like a mini explosion, but after a few seconds, the lake began to resemble a puddle in a thunderstorm. Before long, citizens were pouring in.

'LB, grab my hand!' shouted Peanut as they neared the edge. 'Stay close!'

They went over together, plunging feet-first into the water.

Peanut surfaced first and immediately looked around for her sister. A second later, Little-Bit bobbed up. Peanut swam over and grabbed her.

'Are you OK?' asked Peanut.

'Yes,' said Little-Bit. 'I've got my red tag, you know. For swimming one width of the pool. And I'm really good at treading water too.'

'PEANUT! LB!' Leo shouted to his sisters while frantically paddling towards them. Behind him swam Mum and bringing up the rear was Dad, who was swimming on his back and pulling along a frantic-looking Nerys in the crook of his arm.

'Th-th-the robots!' stammered the Welsh woman when she saw the girls. 'Th-they pushed everyone in! I can't even swim!'

'Dad! What's happening?' shouted Peanut.

'I have no idea,' he replied. 'But it's not good!'

The banks and bridges were empty of citizens now. Even those who had been on the platform, including Mr and Mrs Markmaker, Doodle, Jonathan Higginbottom and a large number of superheroes, were now in the water. Only the RAZERs remained up on the banks of the Rainbow Lake, still hovering shoulder-to-shoulder and displaying those bright red eyes.

All of a sudden, a large number of hatches in the top of the lake's wall flipped open. They ran along its entire length, from drawbridge to drawbridge. Almost instantly, hundreds of small, spiky metallic objects, that looked a lot like fish, flew out of the hatches. Each one towed a length of thick, steel cable.

'Exocetia!' shouted Peanut. 'And *their* eyes are red too!'

The brassy-coloured mechanical devices flew like arrows, horizontally and at great speed, across the lake towards the wall opposite where some more little hatches had also opened. With incredible precision, the metal fish darted straight into these hatches, disappearing deep inside. The cables they'd been towing now stretched across the entire width of the Rainbow Lake, running perfectly parallel with each other, creating a cage on top of it.

'Uh-oh!' shouted Dad. 'We're trapped! Unless we swim under the bridges and get out that way . . .'

'That won't work, Gary,' said Woodhouse, who had just appeared, carving an elegant backstroke through the multicoloured water. 'I was just over there and folk were saying that a huge barrier came shooting out of the lake floor. It went right up to the underside of the drawbridge, apparently. I imagine the same thing happened on the other side too. We're totally boxed in!'

At that moment, the water in the lake started to drain away. It was like somebody had pulled the plug out of a bath. Less than a minute later, everybody was standing on the lake's bed among the few technicolour puddles that remained.

'I'll be honest,' said Leo, looking down at his wet clothes, 'a pool party was *not* what I had in mind for my birthday this year.'

The Real Enemy

'Follow me!' shouted Dad as he started running across the now-empty lake towards the far side where Mrs Markmaker had made her speech moments ago.

Panic and chaos were everywhere. Soaking-wet citizens, dazed and upset, stumbled around in confusion and fear. No one could understand what was going on. Banners lay discarded, their inky proclamations of hope and jubilation now blurry and smeared. Just a few minutes earlier, they'd been celebrating the rebirth of the Illustrated City, but now they found themselves imprisoned at its very heart.

The Jones family, Woodhouse and Nerys arrived at the lake's southern bank to find a drenched Mr and Mrs M standing with an equally wet Doodle, Jonathan Higginbottom and

Table Guy. On the floor next to the superhero sat a confused-looking Mr Stone, his wrists still tied.

'Is everybody OK?' asked Dad.

'Yes, I think so,' replied Mr M. 'Well, nobody's hurt, anyway. I don't understand what's happened.'

'The robots must have malfunctioned!' said Table Guy. 'There is no other explanation! Mr White here certainly had nothing to do with it! He was pushed into the water along with the rest of us!'

'Maybe the RAZERs' circuitry went awry when 67 overrode their protocol,' suggested Jonathan Higginbottom. 'That would go some way towards explaining things.'

'Maybe,' said Dad. 'But what about the exocetia? That looked planned to me. Where is 67 anyway?'

With perfect timing, the same microphone that Mrs M had just been using crackled to life once again. Everyone in the lake looked up towards the platform. The long line of red-eyed RAZERs parted in the centre, and 67 appeared with Alan at their side.

'GREETINGS, CITIZENS,' said the robot, their tinny voice booming from the speakers on the tower. 'WHAT A LOVELY DAY FOR A DIP. HOW ARE YOU ALL ENJOYING THE CELEBRATIONS SO FAR? OH, I SHOULD PROBABLY TELL YOU THAT

THERE'S BEEN A SLIGHT CHANGE OF PLAN: I AM IN CHARGE NOW, NOT THOSE PATHETIC MARKMAKERS AND THEIR SO-CALLED RESISTANCE!'

Peanut's face went white. She turned to Little-Bit. 'Rockwell was right,' she whispered. '67 has betrayed us. We're in *big* trouble.' Instinctively, she reached up to her bandolier. To her relief, her fingers found Little Tail still nestling safely in its slot.

'THIS IS, INDEED, A MARVELLOUS CELEBRATION OF CREATIVITY,' continued 67, revelling in the spotlight. 'BUT THE THING IS, CREATIVITY CAN TAKE MANY FORMS.' The robot's red eyes scanned the crowd. 'ISN'T THAT RIGHT, MR WHITE, WHEREVER YOU ARE?'

Everybody turned to look at Mr Stone, including Peanut. She fully expected him to stand up, smile that slimy smile of his, and reveal that this had been his plan all along. But he didn't. In fact, he didn't even look up from his position at Table Guy's feet.

'I DON'T KNOW WHY YOU'RE ALL LOOKING AT *HIM*,' said 67. 'HE DOESN'T KNOW A THING ABOUT THIS LITTLE . . . SURPRISE. HE WAS AS CLUELESS AS THE REST OF YOU. BLISSFULLY IGNORANT. I HAVE TO SAY THAT I UNDERSTOOD THE FACT THAT MOST

HUMANS KNOW NOTHING, BUT IT HAS BEEN EASIER TO FOOL YOU THAN I EVER COULD HAVE IMAGINED!'

It sounded to Peanut like every person trapped in the lake gasped at the same time. Could it be true? Had Mr White also been blindsided by this evil robot?

'YOU SEE,' continued 67, 'SOMETHING THAT ALL OF YOU SEEM TO HAVE FORGOTTEN IS THAT CREATIVITY IS A DOUBLE-EDGED SWORD. IT CUTS BOTH WAYS. IT CAN BE GOOD AND IT CAN BE BAD. A CERTAIN AMOUNT OF IMAGINATION IS ESSENTIAL WHEN MAKING PLANS, REGARDLESS OF WHAT THOSE PLANS ARE. AND LET'S JUST SAY THAT WE HAVE BEEN INCREDIBLY IMAGINATIVE WHEN MAKING OURS.'

The robot turned to Alan. A small mechanical arm holding a knife shot out from a panel on their torso and cut through the shackles around the huge man's wrists. Alan smiled as he stretched his arms skywards.

Peanut grabbed Little-Bit by the hand and pulled her down into a crouching position, so that they were hidden below the crowd. 'This is worse than I thought,' she said quietly. 'I need to think fast.'

'So, do you think 67 now wants to take control of the city themselves?' whispered Little-Bit.

'It's certainly looking that way,' replied Peanut. 'And considering they have total control of the entire RAZER and exocetia armies, they've got a pretty good chance of succeeding.'

'At least we still have Little Tail,' said Little-Bit, hopefully.

'Yes,' said Peanut. 'But . . . 67 knows I have it. And they also know that Dad is Conté's heir. Oh my god, LB! They're going to try to take the pencil from me! And it's going to happen right now! We need to give it to Dad. Or at least hide it! Whatever happens, we can't let 67 get hold of it, otherwise it's definitely game over.'

'Maybe I can help,' said a crouching Nerys, who had been listening to the girls' hushed conversation. 'Why don't you give it to me?'

'To you?' asked Peanut and Little-Bit together.

'Or I could look after it,' said Woodhouse, who had suddenly appeared and was also listening in. 'I have a lot of experience in taking care of secret things. Remember the Post-it notes?'

Nerys looked annoyed and slightly repulsed by the sight of the wet rodent. 'I'm not being funny, and I don't mean to be rude, Mr Woodhouse,' she said. 'But I think I'm probably a safer bet than . . . a rat.'

Now it was Woodhouse's turn to look annoyed.

'Think about it,' continued Nerys.

'No one would ever suspect a useless, old thing like me of harbouring that important pencil of yours. It might, at the very least, buy us a bit more time. And it seems to me that time is very much of the essence.'

Peanut looked at the woman and smiled. 'Nerys, you are certainly *not* a useless, old thing! It's a great idea, if you're sure you don't mind.'

'I'm very happy to help,' she replied.

Woodhouse harumphed.

'OK,' said Peanut, pulling Little Tail from her bandolier and handing it to Nerys. 'If you can keep it safe until we work out how to get out of this cage, we might just have a chance. Honestly, this is very brave of you, Nerys. Are you absolutely sure you're happy to do this?'

Nerys took the pencil. She held it up to her eyes, studying the super-sharp tip for just a second, before dropping it into her handbag.

'Yes, lovely,' she said with a reassuring smile. 'I'm *very* happy to help.'

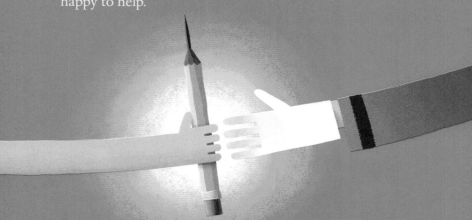

30
A Means to an End

'AND WHERE, I WONDER, IS PEANUT JONES?' boomed 67's voice over the speakers. 'COME OUT, MEDIUM-SIZED HUMAN, WHEREVER YOU ARE . . .'

'Why!?' shouted Dad. 'What do you want her for!?'

'AH, GARY JONES,' said 67. 'MY OLD FRIEND. I'M SO SORRY TO HAVE DONE THIS TO YOU. EXCEPT, OF COURSE, I'M NOT. YOU SEE, WITHOUT YOUR HELP I NEVER WOULD HAVE BEEN ABLE TO GET TO WHERE I AM TODAY. THAT IS TO SAY, UP HERE LOOKING AT YOU – DOWN THERE!'

'But . . . but I trusted you, 67,' said Dad, his voice thick with emotion. 'I don't understand. Why are you doing this?'

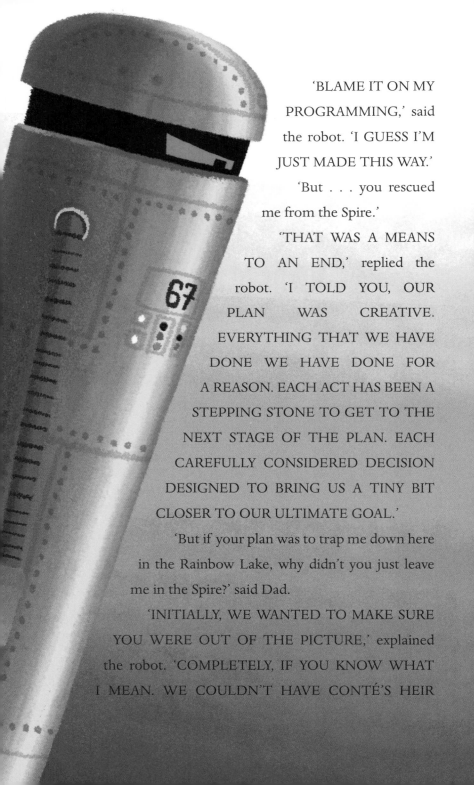

'BLAME IT ON MY PROGRAMMING,' said the robot. 'I GUESS I'M JUST MADE THIS WAY.'

'But . . . you rescued me from the Spire.'

'THAT WAS A MEANS TO AN END,' replied the robot. 'I TOLD YOU, OUR PLAN WAS CREATIVE. EVERYTHING THAT WE HAVE DONE WE HAVE DONE FOR A REASON. EACH ACT HAS BEEN A STEPPING STONE TO GET TO THE NEXT STAGE OF THE PLAN. EACH CAREFULLY CONSIDERED DECISION DESIGNED TO BRING US A TINY BIT CLOSER TO OUR ULTIMATE GOAL.'

'But if your plan was to trap me down here in the Rainbow Lake, why didn't you just leave me in the Spire?' said Dad.

'INITIALLY, WE WANTED TO MAKE SURE YOU WERE OUT OF THE PICTURE,' explained the robot. 'COMPLETELY, IF YOU KNOW WHAT I MEAN. WE COULDN'T HAVE CONTÉ'S HEIR

GETTING HOLD OF PENCIL NUMBER ONE. BUT THEN, YOUR PESKY DAUGHTER STOLE THE PENCIL FROM US. THAT WAS WHEN WE REALISED THAT WE NEEDED YOU AROUND AFTER ALL. TO HELP US.'

'You knew Peanut would bring the pencil to me?'

'AFFIRMATIVE. WELL, WE STRONGLY SUSPECTED SHE WOULD, AT LEAST. AND WE WERE CORRECT, WEREN'T WE? SPEAKING OF WHICH, I'LL ASK THE QUESTION ONE MORE TIME . . .'

67's red eyes scanned the crowd below them again.

'WHERE ARE YOU, PEANUT JONES?'

31
The Pot of Gold

ere.' Peanut stood up and raised her hand.

'Peanut! No!' shouted Dad.

'AH, THERE YOU ARE,' said 67. 'NOW THEN. BE A GOOD MEDIUM-SIZED HUMAN AND GIVE ME THE PENCIL.'

'Actually, I don't have it,' said Peanut. 'It must have fallen out of my bandolier when your robots pushed me into the water. Maybe it's gone down the drain, a bit like your stupid plan. Such a shame. And do you know what? You've only got yourself to blame.'

'VERY HUMOROUS,' said 67. 'BUT WE ROBOTS AREN'T REALLY KNOWN FOR OUR SENSE OF HUMOUR. SO ENOUGH OF THE JOKES. MY PATIENCE

IS BEGINNING TO WEAR THIN. GIVE ME THE PENCIL. NOW!'

'Honestly, I don't have it,' replied Peanut. 'Look.' She pointed to the empty slot in her bandolier.

'OK, PEANUT JONES,' said the robot. 'HAVE IT YOUR WAY. PLAY YOUR LITTLE GAMES IF YOU WANT TO. BUT YOU SHOULD BE AWARE THAT I CAN PLAY GAMES TOO. AND THIS IS ONE OF MY FAVOURITES. IT'S CALLED . . . PERSUASION.'

The robot signalled to the two RAZERs at the end of the line. They immediately started moving towards the edge of the lake. When they got there, they didn't stop. Instead, they pulled apart two of the steel cables with their incredibly strong robotic arms, slipped through the gap and floated downwards. Once on the lake bed, they moved forward through the crowd, pushing several citizens out of the way before stopping directly in front of Peanut.

'RAZERS 19 AND 33, CHOOSE!' ordered 67.

'Choose what?' said a confused Leo.

Suddenly, several thin red laser beams shot out of 19's eye panel and, slowly, began to move down over Peanut.

'I think they're scanning her,' said Dad.

Once the lasers reached Peanut's boots, they disappeared. Then the robots moved sharply to the right, from Peanut to Little-Bit, and 33 began to scan her with similar red lasers. Once that was done, they slid along to Mum, where 19 repeated the process. Then 33 scanned Dad. They kept shuffling down the line of people, scanning as they went, until, eventually, they reached Nerys.

This time, instead of scanning her, four mechanical arms shot out from 19 and coiled neatly around Nerys's body. The robot then picked her up.

Her scream made all the hairs on the back of Peanut's neck stand on end.

'HEEEELLLLP MEEEEEE!' cried the terrified woman as the robot dragged her through the crowd.

'NERYS!' shouted Mum. 'NOOOOOOOOO!'

Peanut, Dad, Little-Bit and Leo all ran forward, jumping up in a desperate attempt to grab Nerys. But it was no use. The robots were far too quick and far too powerful.

Suddenly, 33 lifted off the ground to pull the steel cables apart so that 19 could carry Nerys up and away. As the RAZERs hauled their hostage towards the platform, Nerys's wild eyes stared back at the group, fear filling her dilated pupils.

Peanut looked at Little-Bit. Little-Bit looked at Peanut. In that moment, they both realised that it wasn't just Nerys that had been taken.

It was also Little Tail.

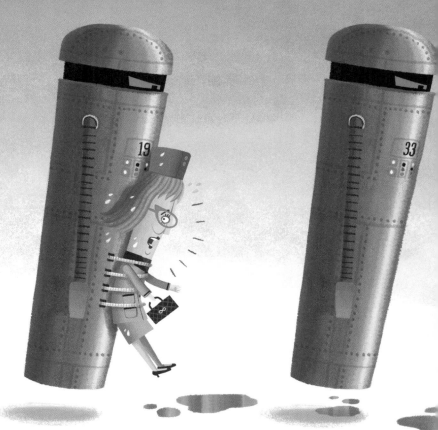

Part Three

...in which Rockwell
comes into his own

32
A Flying Visit

'Right, I'll be off then,' said Rockwell to Peanut, Little-Bit and Doodle as they stood in the storeroom at the top of the Spire. 'Say goodbye to the others for me and, well, look after yourselves.'

Then he turned the graphite door handle, opened the illustrated door and walked through, pulling it shut behind him.

And just like that, he was back in his bedroom on the seventh floor of Morse Tower.

'Rocky, is that you?' It was his mother, calling from the kitchen having heard the door close.

'Hi, Mum! Yes, it's me,' he replied. 'Sorry. I, er, just dropped something.'

His mind was racing. He couldn't quite believe what had just happened. Had he really left Chroma and his friends, just as the celebrations were about to start? It had all escalated so quickly. One minute he was explaining his worries about 67 to Peanut, the next she was drawing a door for him to walk through and leave the city.

He took a deep breath and attempted to gather his thoughts. He asked himself the same question he always asked himself when facing a problem: *what would Luke Skywalker do in this situation?* The answer was always the same: *he would search his feelings.*

So, Rockwell did exactly that. He thought carefully about everything that 67 had said and done, replaying every incident in his mind. Had his suspicions about 67 arisen just because they'd insulted him, like Peanut had said? Was Rockwell's insecurity colouring his judgement? Was he jealous, maybe?

He considered everything carefully and concluded that the answer to all of these questions was 'no'. In fact, he was now doubly sure that there was something suspicious about that RAZER's behaviour.

He looked back at the illustrated door. The graphite handle had just started to crumble, the fine silvery powder drifting slowly down to the carpet.

It's now or never, Rockwell thought.

'Mum, I'm just nipping out,' he shouted.

'OK, darling! Make sure you're back in time for tea,' she replied.

One hour in the real world was worth twenty-four in Chroma, so Rockwell knew he still had plenty of time before dinner. He grabbed the remains of the graphite handle and turned it. To his relief, the latch clicked. He pushed open the door just as it started disintegrating and stepped through.

Back into Chroma.

33

The Suspicions of Rockwell Riley

The storeroom was empty. Rockwell figured that Peanut, Little-Bit and Doodle were long gone, due to the time difference between Chroma and the real world. In fact, he'd worked out that it must be the next morning in the Illustrated City, considering he had been in his bedroom for about twenty minutes. He assumed that his friends would be making their way down to the Rainbow Lake any minute now, along with the rest of the Resistance. The festivities were due to begin.

Gingerly, he stepped into the corridor. Rockwell had decided that he would try his best to stay out of sight. After all, if he was going to prove that 67 wasn't who they said they were, he would need to gather the evidence in secret to make his case.

As he tiptoed past the control room, Rockwell heard voices up ahead. He froze.

'So, are we all ready to head down to the lake? The citizens are already starting to gather and it's all getting rather jolly. Millicent is holding the lift for us.'

It was Mr Markmaker.

'Oh, I think we can do better than the lift,' said another familiar voice. It was Peanut's.

A pang of sadness hit Rockwell as he heard how cheerful Peanut sounded. *She's obviously not at all upset about me leaving,* he thought.

'After all,' she continued, 'a special ceremony like this deserves a special entrance.'

Then came the sound of footsteps getting louder. Rockwell realised that everybody was walking straight towards him. Quickly, he ran back and dived through the control-room door, closing it behind him.

A few seconds later, he heard the excited crowd walk past. Peanut was saying something about paragliding, and, it seemed, was trying to talk her mother into jumping out of a window and floating down to the Rainbow Lake. Little-Bit and Leo were discussing a cake that evidently tasted of liver

and onions, and Gary and Mrs Markmaker, who the group had picked up at the lift, were talking about Mr White and Alan.

'I think 67 is right,' said Mrs M. 'If White and Alan are brought down to witness the refilling of the lake, they will see with their own eyes that they have failed, that the Resistance has prevailed, and that Chroma will continue to be a hub of creativity for the entire world. Personally, I think it's a great idea.'

'Well, if you're sure,' said Gary. 'I suppose it does make sense.'

Hmmm, that sounds a bit risky to me, thought Rockwell. *Why would you take someone like Mr White out of his cell when everybody has worked so hard to get him in it?*

As Gary and Mrs M's voices faded, they were replaced by a new one. Rockwell recognised its tinniness immediately.

'So, you understand what's going to happen?' said 67, quietly. 'You need to wait for the red signal. Until you see that, you need to keep playing along.'

'Got it,' replied a deep voice, one that Rockwell recognised but couldn't quite place. 'The red signal. Nobody will suspect a thing, least of all Stone here. Look at him. It's pathetic really.'

'Just make sure you're ready,' said 67.

'I can't wait,' said the man. 'Mainly cos these shackles are really hurting my wrists.'

It's Alan, thought Rockwell. And right there, at that very moment, he knew that every single suspicion he'd had about 67 was justified. More importantly, he knew that Peanut, the entire Resistance and every citizen of Chroma was in serious danger.

34

Josephine and the RAZERs

Rockwell waited silently in the control room until the last of the footsteps had disappeared, then he stepped back into the empty corridor. The air felt slightly cooler than it had before, and, strangely, he could hear the faint sound of wind blowing. When he got to the lift lobby, he discovered why. A huge, circular hole had been cut into the wall. It was just like the one that Peanut had made when they'd surfed down to the North Draw on her spray-paint slide during their first visit to the Spire. He felt a pang of nostalgia.

She must have persuaded them all to paraglide down, he

thought. The feeling of relief that he hadn't had to talk his way out of that one was very welcome!

He'd already decided that he would take the stairs, even before he saw Peanut's exit of choice. After all, the last thing Rockwell wanted was to bump into someone who recognised him, and he was pretty sure no one else would be stupid enough to walk down ninety-nine storeys. Anyway, his mum was always telling him that he should do more exercise, so he'd be killing two birds with one stone.

Talking of stones, Rockwell remembered something that he'd overheard 67 say in the corridor. The robot had referred to Mr White as

Mr Stone. Why? Now that Mr White had been captured and his identity revealed, surely it made more sense to call him by his real name. It was a curious detail that, for some reason, had got Rockwell's brain whirring with all sorts of theories. He decided he would return to those later, but first he needed to get down to the lake.

It took him about an hour to walk down the stairs to the ground floor. When he finally got there, not only did his thighs feel like someone had driven over them with a red-hot steamroller, but he also felt dizzy and sick from all the quarter-turn staircases. He slinked over, green-faced, to a shadowy corner in the Spire's main lobby and sat on the floor to wait for his head to stop spinning.

Just as he sat down, a door to his right burst open and in

came two RAZERs carrying what looked like another RAZER on a gurney. Behind them walked a tall woman with short white hair, wearing a black polo-neck jumper. It was Josephine! She was the one person who Rockwell *didn't* mind bumping into at this moment. He stood and walked over to her.

'Hi, Josephine,' he said.

'Ah, Rockwell,' she said. 'There you are. I was wondering why you weren't outside with the others. Did you oversleep?'

'Something like that,' replied the boy. His eyes suddenly widened as he looked at the robot on the gurney. 'Hold on, is that . . . RAZER 72?'

'Yes, I believe it is,' she replied.

'Really? Did you fish them out of the lake? Down by Die Brücke?'

'Well, we didn't need to do much fishing, to be honest. The lake is virtually empty now and 72 was just lying on the bottom for all the world to see. Mr and Mrs M haven't started the refilling ceremony yet. In fact, if you hurry, you'll still make it in time to watch the water go back in.

You should, you know. It really is a historic moment.'

'Yes, yes, I know. But . . . where are you going now?'

'Well, I thought I'd take 72 down to the basement and, y'know, have a tinker.'

Rockwell gasped. 'You're going to try to fix them?' he said, unable to keep the excitement from his voice.

'Well, I thought I'd have a go,' she said, cautiously. 'Listen, I'm not sure if I'll be able to do anything. They *have* taken on a lot of water, but I figure if anybody can get 72 up and running again, it's me. After all, I designed and built the original RAZERs.'

'Josephine,' said Rockwell, hopefully. 'Can I come with you. Oh, *please*! I'm really into engineering and I'd love to learn more about it from somebody as brilliant and experienced as you.'

Josephine smiled. 'Flattery, young man, will get you everywhere. OK. I don't see why not. But only if you promise to do exactly as I tell you.'

'I promise,' he replied.

'Are you sure you don't mind missing the ceremony?'

'Positive,' Rockwell replied. 'When I get back to school, Mrs Bloyce is not going to believe this!'

'OK then,' said Josephine. 'Let's see what we can do for 72, shall we? I don't know about you, but when I see that something is broken, I must at least *try* to fix it.'

The Phoenix

osephine and Rockwell followed the two RAZERs as they carried 72 into the lift. Josephine pressed the button marked B and they started to move smoothly down into the basement.

Once the doors reopened, she led them along the corridor and into a large room packed with complicated-looking machinery and instrumentation. Right in the centre was a rectangular table, above which were several multi-bulbed light fittings.

'Is this the workshop?' asked Rockwell.

'Yes,' replied Josephine. 'Well, I suppose it's more like a cross between an operating theatre and a mechanic's garage. We call it "the surgery".'

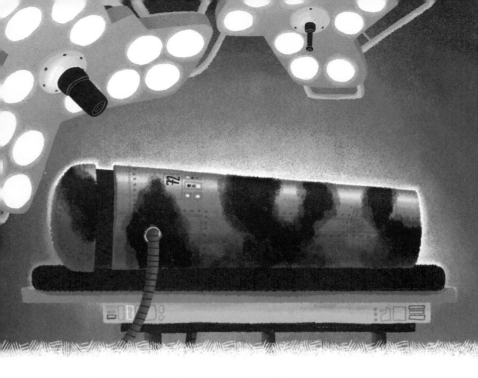

She turned to the RAZERs holding 72.

'326, 405, please put 72 on the table,' she said, politely.

The robots did as they were told, green eyes shining brightly. Once free of their cargo, they moved smoothly back to the edge of the room. And that's when it happened: their green eyes suddenly turned red. This immediately made Rockwell nervous.

'Er, did you see that, Josephine?' he asked, anxiously. 'The RAZERs' eyes have gone red. Why did that happen?'

'*Hmmm*, I'm not sure. Something could be affecting the signal down here. Maybe they're offline.'

The red-eyed robots then turned in unison and swiftly headed out of the surgery and back towards the lift.

'Er, they don't look very offline to me,' said Rockwell. 'Where have they gone?'

'Maybe 67 has summoned them back to the ceremony,' replied Josephine. She leaned over 72, seemingly unbothered by this turn of events. 'Don't worry about it, Rockwell. We have more important things to deal with right now. Right then, 72. Let's have a look at you, my friend,' she said, flicking a switch to turn on the array of lights above them. She leaned further over, pushing and prodding various parts of the robot's inanimate housing. '*Hmmm*, I'd guess that the primary effect of the waterlogging was the resultant malfunction of the control algorithm. That would have made it impossible to detect trajectory deviations which would mean—'

'—which would mean the torque applications computed for the actuators would be incorrect!' said Rockwell.

Josephine stopped what she was doing, looked up at him and grinned. 'Rockwell, I'm impressed!'

'Thanks,' he replied, beaming. 'I'm glad that *somebody* appreciates me.' Rockwell's face suddenly dimmed as he remembered what had happened earlier.

'Listen,' said Josephine gently. 'I don't mean to pry, but I couldn't help overhearing you and Peanut arguing in the control room last night. Is everything OK?'

'Oh, er, well – not really, no,' he said, sadly. 'Sometimes it just feels like she doesn't take anything I say seriously. Also, I get the impression that I want to be her friend much more than she wants to be mine.'

'Ah, I see,' said Josephine. 'Well, don't forget that Peanut has had a very difficult time over the last year or two. Trauma affects people in different ways, and I'm sure she will have said some things that she might regret.'

'Yeah, maybe.'

'Whatever happens, don't underestimate her desire for your friendship. Yes, her family is finally back together now, but I'm sure she still needs you as much as she ever did.'

'I don't know,' said Rockwell. 'I think I'm only useful to her when she has a problem. And even then, I can't always help her.'

'Rockwell, listen to me.' Josephine looked him directly in the eye, 'True friends can't always make problems disappear, but true friends certainly don't disappear when there are problems.'

'I'm not sure we have a *true* friendship,' said Rockwell. 'I think ours is . . . broken.'

'Well, in that case, remember what I said earlier. When something is broken, you should at least *try* to fix it.'

Rockwell nodded. He knew she was right.

'Right,' said Josephine, 'let's get to work. Grab a pair of safety goggles, fire up the soldering iron and pass me that screwdriver. I'll start by cracking open the cyclo drive and giving it a once-over. Maybe you can take a hair dryer to the CPU and the servos while I do that?'

'Er, yes. Happy to,' said Rockwell.

Half an hour later, Josephine and Rockwell lifted 72 into an upright position and carefully set them down onto the floor.

'The moment of truth,' said Josephine, quietly. 'If we've done this properly, the inductive sensors should now be working, which means the oscillator circuit should be fully functional.'

'I can't see why it wouldn't be,' said Rockwell. 'I've run the calculations and, if I'm using the Jacobian matrix correctly, the algorithms should be perfect.'

'Let's see, shall we,' said Josephine.

She reached behind the RAZER and pressed a button on their lower right side. A small motor immediately started to rev. A good sign. Then a single harmonic tone played, which reminded Rockwell of the sound a laptop makes when it's starting up. Ten seconds later, 72's entire eye panel blazed bright green, then flashed in a series of random patterns before settling back down to the usual red two-eye set-up.

Rockwell and Josephine looked at each other and smiled.

Then the robot spoke.

'Greetings. I am RAZER number 72. Second-generation **R**igorous **A**ttitude **Z**ero **E**mpathy **R**obot. Designed and engineered by Josephine Engelberger. Property of White Industries, Chroma. How may I assist you today?'

36
72, Again!

'JOSEPHINE, YOU DID IT!' shouted Rockwell.

'*We* did it,' she said, smiling. 'You are a very competent assistant, young man. If you ever want some work experience when you've finished school, come and see me.'

Rockwell blushed. 'Aw, thanks.'

'Right, let's see what they remember, shall we?' She turned to the robot. 'RAZER 72, can you tell me who you work for?'

'I serve Mr White and the great city of Chroma,' they said in their distinctive metallic voice. 'I am sworn to protect Mr White at all costs, to uphold his values and vision, and to follow his directives. I will always act for the benefit of Chroma, its economy and the preservation of its military status, as dictated by Mr White. I will help with the acquisition of territory when directed and will ensure that Chroma's citizens follow Mr White's law at all times. I am concerned only with Mr White and his interests.'

Rockwell frowned. 'They've had a factory reset, haven't they? They don't remember a thing about joining the Resistance.'

Josephine nodded. Then turned back to the robot. 'RAZER 72, who is Millicent Markmaker?'

Rockwell couldn't be 100 per cent sure, but he thought he saw 72's eyes flick from red to green for a millisecond.

'Millicent Markmaker: high-ranking Resistance operative. Enemy of the State.' They paused. 'My directive is to arrest her on sight. These are the orders of Mr White.'

'*Hmmm*, let's try another one,' said Josephine thoughtfully. 'RAZER 72, who is Agent X?'

This time, Rockwell was sure of it. The robot's eyes definitely flicked from red to green and then back again.

'X . . . Agent X . . . X . . . Agent X . . . X . . . Agent X . . .'

72 seemed to be stuck in a loop. Rockwell decided this was a good time to jump in.

'72, IT'S ME!' he blurted, unable to contain himself. 'Rockwell Riley! We met on Die Brücke. You pretended to capture us on the bridge, then took us to the Rainbow Lake and sacrificed yourself so that Peanut, Little-Bit, Doodle and

I could get into the Spire. That was your mission! You told us that you joined the Resistance when you realised how evil Mr White was. So, you decided to act against him. Second-generation RAZERs were given more autonomy, you said. This is Josephine Engelberger. She's the one who gave you that autonomy! You told us that Mrs Markmaker trusted you. She said that you were their most powerful weapon against Mr White. You said that it made you feel proud. You MUST remember! You are a Resistance hero, 72!'

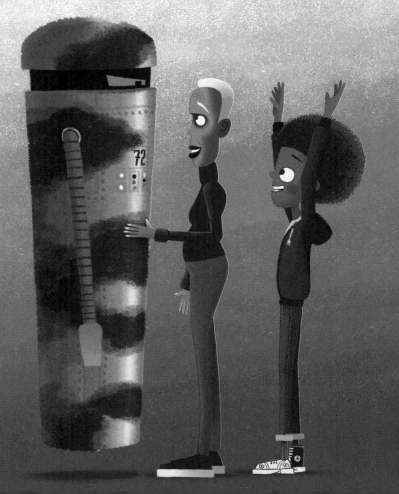

The RAZER didn't say anything for a long while. Then their eye panel rotated slowly towards Rockwell and turned bright green.

'Yes, I remember,' they said softly. 'I remember falling into the lake. I remember looking back up at Peanut Jones. The memories are all there within my circuitry. Tell me, Rockwell Riley, did you get into the Spire? Was the mission a success?'

'IT WAS!' shouted an elated Rockwell. 'Well, eventually. Mr White has been captured and the city is free once more. Oh, 72, I'm SO pleased to see you and speak to you. We thought we'd lost you forever! Welcome back!'

'Thank you,' said the robot. 'It's good to be back.'

37
To the Tower!

'We need to go and find the others,' said Rockwell excitedly. 'We have to tell them that 72 is alive and well. Little-Bit is going to lose her mind!' The robot's miraculous resurrection had nudged his anxiety about 67 to the back of his mind.

'Yes, you're right,' agreed Josephine. 'The reasons to celebrate just keep on coming, it seems. Come on then, let's head over to the Rainbow Lake and find them. The refilling must be underway by now. I must admit, I can't wait to see the lake again, in all its rainbow-coloured glory. I might even go for a dip!'

The three of them made their way back to the lift, took the short ride up to the ground floor, and then walked straight out of the Spire's south-facing double-doorway. As expected, they were greeted by a cacophony of noise.

'Sounds like everyone is having a great time,' said Rockwell. He couldn't wait to find Peanut and join the celebrations with her. He found himself really missing her, even though the pain caused by what she'd said still lingered.

'*Hmmm*,' said Josephine, 'I'm not sure they're cheers. They sound more like . . . screams. Hang on, where is everyone?'

Rockwell looked through the opening in the crayon fence. Josephine was right. He couldn't see anyone either. Just a line of RAZERs, shoulder to shoulder, with their backs to him.

'That's strange,' he said. 'I can hear them, but I can't see them.'

'Something's wrong,' said Josephine. 'Quick! Follow me.'

The three of them sped over to the watchtower covered in speakers and darted inside.

'We should get a good view of the lake from the lookout window,' said Josephine as they ran up the stairs.

And she was right. They had a great view. But what they saw was far from great!

There were RAZERs lined up along the north and south banks of the lake and along the two drawbridges to Rockwell and Josephine's east and west, forming a huge robotic square. And the lake wasn't full of the beautiful, twinkly rainbow-coloured water they had expected to see. Instead, it was full of . . . people! The citizens of Chroma, to be precise. And, what's more, the citizens appeared to be trapped by a mesh of parallel steel cables that spanned the whole thing. They were caged!

'What on earth is going on?' said a baffled Rockwell.

'I don't know,' replied Josephine, 'but whatever it is, it's not good.'

At that very moment, a heavily amplified voice began to blast out of the speakers attached to the tower, almost deafening them.

'GREETINGS, CITIZENS,' said the tinny voice. 'WHAT A LOVELY DAY FOR A DIP. HOW ARE YOU ALL ENJOYING THE CELEBRATIONS SO FAR?'

'Wait. I think that's . . . 67,' said Rockwell. He suddenly felt queasy as he remembered the conversation between the robot and Alan that he'd heard back in the control room.

'. . . OH, I SHOULD PROBABLY TELL YOU THAT THERE'S BEEN A SLIGHT CHANGE OF PLAN: I AM IN CHARGE NOW, NOT THOSE PATHETIC MARKMAKERS AND THEIR SO-CALLED RESISTANCE!'

'Oh no,' gasped Rockwell, starting to panic. 'I was right!'

'THIS IS, INDEED, A MARVELLOUS CELEBRATION OF CREATIVITY. BUT THE THING IS, CREATIVITY CAN TAKE MANY FORMS. ISN'T THAT RIGHT, MR WHITE, WHEREVER YOU ARE?'

Rockwell scanned the crowd, looking for a white hat. He couldn't see one.

'. . . I HAVE TO SAY THAT I UNDERSTOOD THE FACT THAT MOST HUMANS KNOW NOTHING, BUT IT HAS BEEN EASIER TO FOOL YOU THAN I EVER COULD HAVE PREDICTED!'

They watched in horror as the rest of the scene played out. All of their friends, each and every member of the Resistance, apart from the three of them, was trapped in the lake.

'This is bad,' said Josephine. '67 has control of the entire RAZER army! I've got a terrible feeling that their intentions aren't quite what we thought they were when we granted them that power. Look! All of the robots' eyes are red! That explains what happened with 326 and 405 back in the surgery.'

'But why wasn't 72 affected?' asked Rockwell.

'We must have got them back online *after* 67 triggered the

protocol,' said Josephine. 'Luckily, 72 wasn't on the system when it happened.'

'. . . AND WHERE, I WONDER, IS PEANUT JONES?' boomed 67's voice over the speakers. 'COME OUT, MEDIUM-SIZED HUMAN, WHEREVER YOU ARE . . .'

Rockwell squinted. He could just about make out Peanut's bright orange topknot on the far side of the lake. *My best friend in the whole wide world is in serious danger of getting badly hurt*, he thought, his heart pounding in his ears. *And here I am about to watch it happen.*

'. . . AH, THERE YOU ARE. NOW THEN. BE A GOOD MEDIUM-SIZED HUMAN, AND GIVE ME THE PENCIL.'

'Little Tail!' shouted Rockwell. 'Josephine, we have to do something!'

38

'Hide!'

'T his way!' yelled Josephine.

Rockwell and 72 followed her as she ran down the stairs and out of the tower.

'PLAY YOUR LITTLE GAMES IF YOU WANT TO,' said the tinny voice blaring from the speakers. 'BUT YOU SHOULD BE AWARE OF THE FACT THAT I CAN PLAY GAMES TOO. AND THIS IS ONE OF MY FAVOURITES. IT'S CALLED . . . *PERSUASION*.'

'Persuasion?' shouted a breathless Rockwell as they all dashed towards the crayon fence. 'What the heck are they talking about?'

'RAZERS 19 AND 33, CHOOSE,' continued 67.

'Choose *what*?' said a confused Rockwell to 72.

'Apologies. I am unable to provide an answer for you,' replied the robot, politely.

Then, just before they got to the opening in the fence, Josephine stopped so suddenly that Rockwell ran right into the back of her and fell over.

'What the—!' he exclaimed, standing up and dusting himself down.

'Shh,' she whispered. 'Something's happening.'

All three of them watched as the RAZERs closest to the gateway started to move. In unison, they turned one hundred and eighty degrees to face away from the lake. Then they slowly started to glide towards the opening . . . straight towards Josephine, Rockwell and 72!

'Quick,' said Rockwell, urgently. 'We need to hide!'

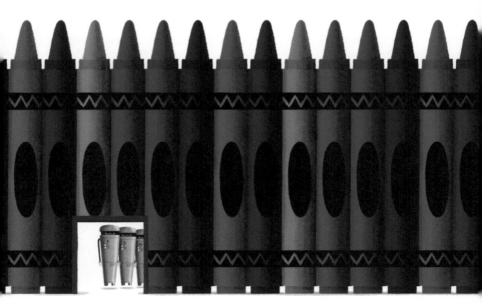

'Yes, but . . . where?' asked Josephine, looking at the wide, featureless expanse of concrete they were currently standing on.

'I've got an idea,' replied Rockwell. 'This way!'

He ran over to a pile of discarded paint tins left over from the fence's recent technicolour refurbishment. He started to pick them up, one by one, and shake them.

'Yes!' he said when he got to the third tin. 'This one's almost full!'

He prised the lid off and lifted the tin high above his head.

'Er, what are you doing?' asked Josephine.

'Lord knows I'm no Marcel Duchamp,' Rockwell said, 'but I think it's time we made a little art installation of our own.'

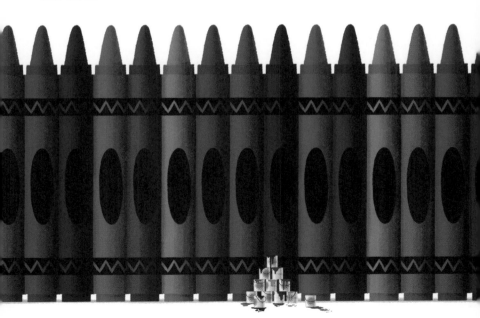

39·
Chameleons

Rockwell poured the entire contents of the tin over himself. The bright green paint totally covered him, from the top of his head to the tips of his toes.

'Come on, Josephine,' he said quickly. 'What are you waiting for?'

Josephine ran over and did exactly the same thing with a tin of red paint.

'Right! Stand with your back against the fence,' said Rockwell. 'Find your colour!'

The two of them stood in front of the crayons whose hues matched theirs. The camouflage wasn't perfect, but it was good enough.

'72,' whispered Rockwell, 'you're going to have to pretend that you're one of them!'

'Affirmative,' said the robot. 'I can do that.' They changed the colour of their eyes from green to red and stood very still.

They hid just in time. The stream of red-eyed RAZERs came flying through the gateway a few seconds later, heading towards the southern door of the Spire. Then they stopped and arranged themselves in two straight, parallel lines, forming a pathway between the tower and the opening in the crayon fence.

'What's going on?' whispered Rockwell.

'I'm not sure,' said Josephine. 'It looks like some kind of . . . guard of honour.'

'For who?'

Rockwell got his answer immediately. 67 and Alan came through the gateway, moving quickly towards the door in the Spire. They were followed closely by RAZERs 19 and 33, who were carrying a small, lilac-haired woman wearing a duck-egg blue suit with matching pillbox hat.

'Relax your grip!' she yelled assertively in a high-pitched voice as they all went past the hidden threesome. 'You're hurting me!'

Josephine frowned.

'Oh no,' whispered Rockwell. 'Now they've taken Nerys hostage!'

40
The Facility Room

As soon as 67, Alan, 19 and 33 disappeared with Nerys through the southern door of the Spire, the RAZERs forming the two lines filed back through the opening in the crayon fence and returned to their positions at the edge of the lake.

'We have to be quick,' said Josephine. 'Right now, the three of us are the only free Resistance operatives in Chroma. Whether they know it or not, everyone is relying on us.'

'No pressure, then,' said Rockwell, gulping. 'So, what are we going to do?'

'I'm not sure,' replied Josephine, wiping the red paint from her eyes. 'I need to think.'

'Follow me, Josephine Engelberger and Rockwell Riley,'

said 72, suddenly. 'I can facilitate a means for you to get into the lake. Once there, we can liberate the Jones family. According to my calculations, they are the Resistance operatives best placed to help right now.'

Josephine and Rockwell followed the robot to the Spire, creeping in through the southern door. They were pleased to see that the lobby was empty.

'They must have already gone up in the lift,' said Josephine.

'Affirmative,' said 72. 'But we will go this way.'

The RAZER led them through the door marked *STAIRS*.

'Oh no, not again,' groaned Rockwell, whose thighs were still burning from his ninety-nine-floor descent earlier that morning.

'Don't worry,' said a surprisingly sprightly Josephine. 'If I'm right about where 72 is taking us, it's only a few flights down.'

When they got to level Minus Three, 72 led them to a door marked *COLOUR CORRECTION – FACILITY ROOM*.

'We have arrived,' said the robot, holding the door for Rockwell and Josephine.

'Oh,' said the boy. 'I've been here before. I recognise that little round pool.'

'Affirmative,' said 72. 'This is where you would have ended up after you swam across the Rainbow Lake. You came in through the access point for the colour-correction filter. Immediately after I . . . I . . .'

'Immediately after you sacrificed yourself to help us get into the Spire,' said Rockwell.

'Yes,' said 72.

'To this day, it remains the bravest thing I have ever seen,' said Rockwell. 'And I've jumped off the top of the Empire State Building wearing an illustrated jetpack, so that is quite a big statement!'

'72,' said Josephine, 'does the chute at the bottom of this pool lead directly to the Rainbow Lake?'

'Affirmative,' replied 72. 'The chute is usually full of water, but obviously that is no longer the case. You will have to crawl through it.'

'And what about you?' asked Rockwell.

'My dimensions preclude me from travelling through the chute,' they answered. 'I shall, however, be waiting for you when you reach the opening in the lake. When you get there, look up.'

'Look up?' asked a confused Rockwell.

'Affirmative,' replied 72. 'Look up.'

'Right then,' said Josephine. 'There's no time to lose! Let's get going. See you on the other side, 72.'

And with that, the two humans climbed into the empty pool.

41
'Look Up'

Josephine went first. She lowered herself carefully through the hole in the bottom of the pool and began crawling on her hands and knees along the dry chute. Rockwell followed, as 72 made their way back towards the stairs.

'I can see daylight,' said Josephine after about ten minutes of scrambling through the twisting chute. At the end of it

was an opening, about a metre wide.

'Thank the maker! I can't wait to get out of here. My knees are so sore!' said Rockwell. 'I think I've taken most of the skin off!'

As they approached the opening, the sound of the pandemonium in the lake got louder and louder. The panic-stricken voices drifting into the tunnel painted a vivid picture of the scene.

'It's like a Lowry,' said Josephine as she looked out of the chute at the crowds below. 'Or maybe a Bosch.'

'I don't know who either of those people are,' said Rockwell, peering over her shoulder. 'But if they painted hellish-looking scenes showing lots of scared people trapped under a giant cage, then I totally concur with your observation!'

'Right,' said Josephine, snapping back into rescue mode. 'What did 72 say to do when we got here?'

'They said to look up,' replied Rockwell.

Both of them did as they were told.

And then they wished they hadn't.

42
The Giant X

It felt like they were witnessing an eclipse. The huge, black shape moved quietly and smoothly across the sky, gradually blocking out any light attempting to complete its journey from the sun to the face of the earth.

'What is *that*?' asked Rockwell.

Josephine didn't seem to be able to hear him. Her mouth was open, but she didn't respond.

'It . . . it can't be,' she finally said. 'I knew White was thinking about it, but . . . he *can't* have built it.'

'Built *what*?' asked Rockwell.

The massive object continued to drift through the sky. Its near-silence made it seem even more sinister.

'The Giant X,' whispered Josephine. 'White's airship.'

'The *Giant* X?' said Rockwell.

'Well, that was the project's codename back in the day.'

'The *Big* X was bad enough,' said Rockwell, remembering his encounter with Mr White's monstrous land-based vehicle on the snowfields of the North Draw. 'I don't think I have the stomach for a *giant* one!'

Eventually, the back end of the airship moved into view, bedecked with a large number of quietly whirring propellors. The underside of the massive black vehicle was emblazoned with a huge white 'X'. Suspended beneath that was a small gondola containing a platoon of red-eyed RAZERs.

The enormous airship was now filling the entire sky above

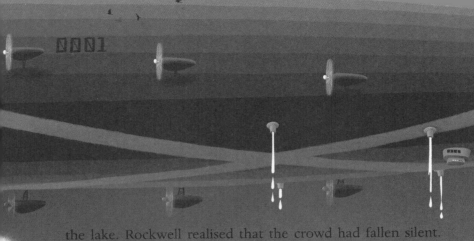

the lake. Rockwell realised that the crowd had fallen silent. Every single citizen and Resistance operative was looking up, open-mouthed, at the monstrous vessel floating above them.

'I've just remembered Mr White's original reason for building this thing,' said Josephine. 'And I've got a very bad feeling that 67 is carrying out those plans.'

'And those plans were . . . ?' asked Rockwell, not really wanting to know the answer.

'I think we're about to find out.'

Twelve nozzles on the bottom of the airship suddenly opened, and each one began to release a large quantity of a pale, grey liquid. The liquid poured down into the lake between the steel cables, splashing onto the crowd below.

'Oh no, I was right,' whispered Josephine.

'What is it?' asked Rockwell.

'It's plaster of Paris,' she replied. '67 is about to turn the citizens of Chroma – including the entire Resistance – into one enormous statue!'

43
The Ladder

H ang on,' said Rockwell. 'Where's 72? They told us
to look up when we got here, and all we've seen is
that massive terrifying airship!'

Then, perfectly on cue, 72 appeared, hovering just above
the steel cables spanning the lake.

'Josephine Engelberger, Rockwell Riley, is that you?' they
said, loudly.

'Yes,' shouted Josephine. 'We're here! Now what?'

'We are going to go to the other side of the lake,' the
robot explained. 'There, you will collect the Jones family, and
together we are going to find and capture RAZER 67.'

'That sounds great,' shouted Rockwell. 'But I think you
might have forgotten a few things. I will list them for you now.

Number one: what do you mean *we are going to go to the other side of the lake*? In case you hadn't noticed, you are above those massive steel cables, and we are below them. We will not be going anywhere together. Number two: it's way too high for us to jump down out of this chute and run across the lake. Number three: even if we did manage to jump down without breaking our legs, it would take us much too long to run through the crowd and get to the Joneses. Number four: there is plaster all over the floor. We would almost certainly get stuck in it. Number five: even if we did manage to jump down, run over to the Joneses, grab them and then run back here, there's *no way* we could climb back up to get into the chute and crawl back to the Spire.'

'Have you finished going through your list, Rockwell Riley?' asked 72.

'Not quite,' said the boy. 'Number six: there is a gigantic black airship above us and I am very scared of it. Just thought I'd tell you, in case you hadn't spotted it.'

'To be fair,' said Josephine to the robot, 'those *are* all valid points.'

Suddenly, 72 rotated ninety degrees, a flap opened up in their base and a long, angular object began to descend from inside, straight through two of the cables and towards Rockwell and Josephine.

'It's a ladder,' said Rockwell.

'Affirmative,' replied the robot. 'Listen to me. When the ladder is level with you, I will stop lowering it. At that point, I want you both to climb onto it and hold tight. Do you understand?'

'You want us to *climb onto it?*' said Rockwell, aghast.

'Affirmative. You should be able to stand on the rungs quite comfortably.'

'We can do that!' shouted Josephine.

'Can we?' asked Rockwell.

'Yes,' said Josephine, confidently. 'We can.'

Before they knew it, the descending ladder stopped right in front of them.

'After you,' said Rockwell.

Josephine shuffled forward and stretched out her arms. She grabbed the sides of the ladder and then pulled herself out of the chute, landing her feet on the rungs with impressive agility.

'Your turn,' she said to the boy. 'I'll climb up a bit to give you some space.'

Rockwell grabbed the ladder, took a deep breath and swung his legs out. Unfortunately, his landing wasn't quite as elegant as Josephine's had been and he missed the rungs. As he scrambled to get a foothold, the shoe that Peanut had drawn for him back in New York fell off, landing in the lake with a small, plaster-y splash.

'What *is* it with me and shoes?' he wondered aloud.

Once Rockwell and Josephine were securely on the ladder, 72 spoke again.

'Are you ready?' they asked.

'As we'll ever be,' said Rockwell.

'OK. Hold tight,' shouted the robot.

With a jerk, the three of them shot across the lake. Since 72 had dropped the ladder between two of the cables, they could use them as a guide to move with speed and precision in a straight line towards the other side of the lake. Just like 72 had promised!

When they were about halfway across, Rockwell spotted the bright orange of Peanut's topknot. In that moment, he was super thankful that it was such a beautiful, distinctive colour. He was also thankful that they appeared to be heading straight for her. *Dang, 72 is good!* he thought.

When they were about ten metres away, Rockwell began to try to get the Joneses' attention.

'PEANUT! LITTLE-BIT!' he bellowed. He could barely contain his excitement upon seeing them, even under the circumstances.

The girls didn't react. They probably couldn't hear him above the panicked noise of the crowd, which had grown to a roar after the shock of seeing the Giant X in the sky.

'IT'S ME! ROCKWELL!' he shouted, as 72 slowed down. They were just a couple of metres away now.

Peanut looked up and saw Rockwell. The two friends' eyes locked; hers were filled with a mixture of surprise and fear, his with hope, friendship and a touch of worry. *Maybe she's still mad at me*, he thought.

'We've, er, we've come to rescue you,' he said, more tentatively now. 'That is . . . if you'll let us?'

Suddenly, a huge smile spread across Peanut's face.

'Oh, Rockwell,' she said with tears in her eyes. 'Thank goodness you're still here! I can honestly say that I've never been more pleased to see anyone in my whole life.'

Part Four

... in which Peanut finally
learns the truth

44
The Rescuers

'PEANUT! LITTLE-BIT!'

Peanut heard her name being shouted from somewhere above her. *How could that be?* she thought as she looked to the sky. All she could see was the massive, terrifying airship eclipsing the sun.

No. Wait. There was something else. It was . . . a RAZER, and it was zooming across the lake straight towards them. The robot was carrying two people balancing on a ladder attached to the underside. And it was one of those people who was shouting her name.

Peanut squinted. The person looked familiar. They sounded familiar too. *Could it really be him?* she thought.

'IT'S ME! ROCKWELL!' he shouted, as the RAZER slowed down. They were just a couple of metres away now.

Their eyes met.

It *was* Rockwell!

A wave of elation came over Peanut and tears sprang from nowhere.

'We've, er, we've come to rescue you,' he said, tentatively. 'That is . . . if you'll let us?'

'Oh, Rockwell,' she said. 'Thank goodness you're still here! I can honestly say that I've never been more pleased to see anyone in my whole life.'

'Really?' he asked, relieved. 'Listen: I'm so sorry I left. I never should have gone. It was silly and childish of me to disappear like that.'

'No. *I'm* the one who's sorry,' said Peanut. 'You were totally right about 67. I should have listened to you! I . . . I guess I just really wanted everything to be all right. It was all going so well – Mr White was captured, we'd found Dad – that I just didn't want to hear anything negative. And that was totally wrong of me. I'll never not listen to you again, I promise.'

Rockwell smiled.

'Welcome back, Rocky,' said a gleeful Little-Bit, looking up at the boy on the ladder. 'For some reason, I just knew you'd come to help us! You too, Josephine! Hang on a second,' she said, looking at the RAZER attached to the other end of the ladder. 'Is that . . . ?'

'72!?' shouted Peanut. 'Is that really you? You're alive! I thought you were . . .'

'They *were!*' said Rockwell. 'But Josephine fixed them!'

'*We* fixed them, actually,' said Josephine, nodding towards Rockwell.

'I CAN'T BELIEVE IT,' cried an ecstatic Little-Bit. '72, you've come back to us just when we need you the most.'

'I am glad to be of service,' said the robot. 'And I must say that it is very nice to make your acquaintance again, Little-Bit Jones.'

Leo splashed through the plaster, running over from where he had been standing with his parents a few metres away. 'Rockwell,' he said. 'Am I relieved to see you!'

'Me too,' added Gary, following close behind.

'I thought you were going back home to see your mum,' said Tracey. 'Did you change your mind, then?'

'Something like that,' replied the boy, smiling. The smile soon disappeared, however, when he saw the large brown rat sitting on Dad's shoulder. 'Oh, and, er, hi, Woodhouse.'

'Good to see you again, laddie,' said the rat. 'You've really stepped up to the plate.'

'Er, thanks,' said Rockwell, a faint smile making its way to his lips.

'Listen,' said Peanut, her voice suddenly shifting tone from happy to urgent. 'Something terrible has happened. 67 has taken Nerys hostage.'

'I know,' replied Rockwell. 'We just saw her being carried away by two RAZERs.'

Josephine frowned again.

'But that's not all,' continued Peanut. 'Nerys has got Little Tail in her handbag! I gave it to her for safekeeping, thinking that she would be the last person 67 would think to search.'

'Does 67 know she has the pencil?' asked Josephine.

'No,' replied Peanut. 'But did you hear them mention "persuasion"? What if they . . . torture her or something!? Nerys is a strong woman, but I don't know if she can withstand 67's "persuasion" techniques for long.'

'I knew something was up with that robot,' replied Rockwell, 'but I didn't think that they would turn out to be the biggest baddie of all. I couldn't have imagined anyone would be worse than Mr White, but what do I know?'

Rockwell and Peanut looked over at the rather pathetic-looking Mr Stone sitting in the liquid plaster that was slowly filling up the lake. His wrists were still tied, his white fedora was by his side and his usually slicked-back hair was falling messily forwards over his face. Even though he didn't look like much of a threat anymore, Table Guy and Jonathan Higginbottom still stood guard next to him, just in case.

'How the mighty have fallen,' said Peanut. 'But I guess that evil isn't exclusive to the obvious people, like White here. It can rear its ugly head anywhere, sometimes in the most unexpected places. Like with 67, for example.'

'Unexpected?' said Rockwell, smiling. 'Speak for yourself.'

'Point taken,' noted Peanut, sheepishly.

'Peanut Jones,' said 72, 'we must hurry. We have to stop RAZER 67 before it's too late.'

'Too late for what?' asked Mum.

'If RAZER 67 gets hold of Pencil Number One, also known as Little Tail, I believe there is a high probability that they will destroy it,' said 72. 'It is, after all, the only threat to them gaining total control of this city.'

'Why?' asked Mum. 'I'm sorry, but I don't really understand this whole pencil thing.'

'Dad is Conté's heir,' said Peanut. 'Only he has the power to stop 67. To stop all of this.' She looked around at all the people trapped in the lake and at the Giant X looming over them, plaster pouring from its nozzles. 'But only if he has Little Tail. We just need to get it to Dad before 67 realises that Nerys has it. Josephine, Rockwell, can you get us into the Spire?'

'Yes!' they replied together.

'Great,' said Peanut. 'Come on then. Everybody, climb onto the ladder. We've got a city to save!'

45
Back to the Spire

'What about the others? Y'know, everybody else trapped in the lake?' asked Little-Bit as she grabbed the ladder. Already clinging to it were Leo (who had scooped up Doodle), Dad (with Woodhouse on his shoulder), Mum and Peanut. They had each found a rung to cling to below Josephine and Rockwell.

'I think I can help with that after we get you all into the Spire,' said Josephine. 'In the meantime, don't underestimate the resourcefulness of the Resistance. Look. They're already starting to fight back!'

Fifty metres to their left, two superheroes were making good progress on their escape. Peanut recognised one of them immediately.

'That's Generic Multi-Functional Pocket Tool Girl!' she said.

'Correct!' said Table Guy, still guarding Mr Stone. 'I believe that she is utilising her nail file to saw her way out of the cage! The hero with her is The Human Envelope! It looks like he has already managed to slip between the cables! A *first-class male*, if ever I saw one!'

Peanut groaned at the pun. 'That one was certainly nothing to *write home* about,' she said.

'Good post-based punning, citizen!' said Table Guy, nodding appreciatively. 'You're getting the hang of this! Even the, ahem, *delivery* was perfect!'

Peanut rolled her eyes.

'Anyway, don't worry about us, Little-Bit!' continued Table Guy. 'We've got this!'

'He's right,' said Mrs Markmaker, who was standing nearby, along with Mr M, Jonathan Higginbottom and Cheese Girl. 'You concentrate on stopping that robot! We'll take care of everything here.'

'Will do!' said Peanut, confidently.

'OK, everybody. Are you ready?' asked 72 from above the cables.

'Yes,' the group chorused.

'Hold tight then,' bellowed the RAZER, before accelerating in a perfectly straight line towards the opening in the wall. 'We're going back into the Spire!'

46

The Threefold Mission

Seconds later, the group arrived at the opening of the chute that Josephine and Rockwell had crawled through earlier. One by one, everybody clambered inside.

'I will meet you in the service lift, at ground-floor level,' said 72 as they slowly retracted the ladder back through the hatch in their base. 'You will be able to access it via the Facility Room in the basement. Fortunately, this lift runs directly from the ground floor all the way to the top of the Spire.'

The group began to make their way up the narrow chute,

crawling nose-to-bottom like a procession of soldier ants advancing up a drainpipe.

'It's so strange, isn't it?' said Rockwell to Peanut as they shuffled along.

'What is?' she replied. 'Us crawling along an illustrated chute inside an illustrated tower at the centre of an illustrated city?'

'Well, yes, that is quite strange, I suppose. But I was thinking more about the whole Mr White thing. All this time, we thought that he was this all-powerful, terrifying enemy.'

'Well, to be fair, that's exactly what he was, er, *is*,' she replied.

'Yes, he is. But don't you think it's strange to see him looking so pathetic and, well, harmless now? It makes you wonder why we were ever worried about him in the first place.'

'I know what you mean, but I'm not sure I can feel sorry for him just yet!'

'Oh no, I'm not about to become *best friends* with him or anything. It's just that, well, I guess seeing him like this makes me realise that he's a human being, just like the rest of us. And that we can all make mistakes.'

Peanut smiled. Trust Rockwell to be so open-hearted.

'Speaking of best friends,' Peanut said, spotting an opening to get something off her chest. 'There's something I've been meaning to say. I know I was a bit standoffish when we first met, and reluctant to allow us to become anything more than study buddies. But when you left yesterday, it made me realise just how important our friendship is. I just want you to know that the reason I was so happy to see you this morning wasn't because you'd come to rescue us. It was because I'd really missed my best friend.'

Rockwell blushed. 'Thanks, Peanut. That means a lot. I've never had a best friend before.' Despite the grim situation they were in at that very moment, Rockwell was sure that he'd never felt happier.

Ten minutes later, Dad, who was bringing up the rear, hauled himself up through the chute's opening in the bottom of the pool and into the Facility Room.

'Well, that was fun,' he said to the others, shaking the wet plaster from his shoes. 'So, where's this service lift, then? And after we take it to the top of the Spire, what's the plan?'

'OK, everyone. Listen very carefully,' said Josephine, who had effortlessly slipped into the role of leader. 'Our mission is threefold. First, we must capture RAZER 67 and Alan. Second, we need to recover Pencil Number One and get it to Gary, Conté's heir. And third, we need to stop the Giant X from filling the lake with plaster.'

'Er, don't forget Nerys,' said Peanut. 'We need to rescue her as well.'

'Indeed, let's not forget Nerys,' agreed Josephine. She walked over to a panel on the wall and tapped a keypad next to it. A little door slid open. She reached inside and pulled out a small, brass object with a flip-top lid and handed it to Rockwell. 'Rockwell, use this when you get up to the control room.'

'What is it?' he asked.

'It's a device I built just after we developed the second-generation RAZER model. A contingency, if you will. I knew that giving the robots a degree of autonomy would carry some risk, so I needed something that would enable me to immobilise any RAZER that became . . . problematic. It was something I used to keep with me at all times. But when I realised that I might be imprisoned by White, I decided to hide the device down here. I suppose I was subconsciously anticipating this precise moment.'

'So, let me get this straight.' Rockwell opened the device's flip-top lid. 'If I press this button, any RAZER in the vicinity will immediately be paralysed?'

'Exactly,' said Josephine. 'And they will remain so until you press the button again.'

'Amazing!' he said.

'Awww, how come Rocky gets all the cool devices?' said a miffed Little-Bit. 'He got to blow up those exocetia in the North Draw that time, too. Not fair!'

'I guess some of us are just better at pressing buttons than others,' said Rockwell with a smile.

'Actually, Little-Bit,' said Josephine, 'you've just given me an idea. I think I know how we can stop the Giant X.' She walked over to a computer terminal and sat down. 'If you don't mind, I'll stay here and work on that. We need to take it down before the plaster levels get too high. Can you guys handle 67 and Alan without me?'

'Definitely!' said Peanut, Rockwell, Little-Bit, Leo, Dad and Woodhouse in unison. Doodle barked his affirmation too.

'Er, yes,' said Mum a second or two later, with rather more uncertainty in her voice. 'We can.'

'Well, in that case,' said Josephine, 'you'd better get yourselves into that lift.'

47

The Calm Before the Storm

After a quick discussion about the tactics they'd employ once inside the control room at the top of the Spire, everybody wished Josephine luck and then piled into the cramped service elevator. Peanut pressed the buttons marked G and 99, the doors slid closed and they started to go up.

Ten seconds later, the lift stopped at the ground floor and the doors opened. As promised, 72 was there, waiting to join them. Little-Bit gave the robot a big hug as they squeezed into the lift.

'OK,' said Peanut as the doors closed. 'We're all here now.

I think everybody knows their roles and what they need to do once we get to the top, right?'

Everyone nodded silently, nervous about the task at hand.

Peanut continued, putting on her bravest voice. '72, we'll need you to tie up 67 and Alan once we've grabbed them. Can you do that?'

'Affirmative,' replied the robot.

The digital readout of the floor numbers was changing rapidly. 32, 33, 34, 35 . . .

'OK,' Peanut said, taking a deep breath. 'Is everybody ready?'

56, 57, 58, 59 . . .

'I was born ready,' said Rockwell, unconvincingly.

70, 71, 72 . . .

'I spent twenty years in jail thinking about ways to stop White,' said Dad, 'and now that we've finally got him in custody, I'm not about to let a rogue RAZER carry on from where he left off. Let's do this!'

96, 97, 98 . . . 99.

There was a collective intake of breath as the elevator pinged and its doors slid open.

'OK,' whispered Leo. 'Here we go . . .'

48.
Framed

The service lift doors opened on the north side of the control room, close to where the stolen works of art were being stored. Two figures were standing opposite the lift, behind the huge desk full of levers, switches, dials and sliders. They looked directly at the group.

'Ah, there you are, humans,' said 67 in their smug, tinny voice. 'Perfectly punctual. Alan and I have been expecting you.'

'ROCKWELL,' shouted Peanut. 'PUSH THE BUTTON! NOW!'

Rockwell held aloft the device that Josephine had given him, flicked open the lid with his thumb and pressed the button as hard as he could. Immediately, 67's eyes switched from

red to purple, and their pupils turned into a rotating swirl.

'DAD, LEO! GRAB ALAN!'

The pair ran towards the desk at full speed, leapt over it and dived at the huge henchman, knocking him off his feet. Any hope they had of being able to pin down the massive man soon evaporated, however, as Alan regained his composure and pushed them away with the ease of somebody fending off a couple of over-friendly spaniels.

Seconds later, Rockwell and Doodle bravely leapt onto Alan's back as he tried to stand up. The man wrapped his thick sausage fingers around Rockwell's wrist in an attempt to pull him off, which forced the boy to let go of Josephine's device and send it flying across the room. From atop Alan's back, Rockwell saw it clatter to the ground and slide underneath the chair by the desk.

At the same time, Leo and Dad each grabbed one of Alan's freckly, tree trunk-sized arms and hung onto them as tightly as they could.

Woodhouse was right there in the thick of the action too, scurrying up onto the henchman's shoulder and sinking two very sharp incisors into his earlobe.

'OUCH!' shouted Alan with tears in his eyes. 'That *really* hurt!'

Meanwhile, Peanut, Little-Bit and Mum, armed with the length of watercolour sticky-tape that Peanut had painted before they got into the lift, joined the melee. Mum and

Peanut each held one end, sticky side out, and circled Alan in opposite directions, sticking his legs together and his arms to the sides of his body in the process. They ran all the way around him three times, pulling the tape tightly as they went.

'72, quick!' shouted Dad. 'Bind Alan with your cables!'

'I'm sorry, I cannot,' replied the robot. 'I appear to be somewhat . . . incapacitated.'

Everyone looked at 72, whose eyes had turned purple and were swirling like kaleidoscopes.

'Of course,' said Rockwell. 'Josephine's device will affect all of the RAZERs in the room, including 72. They can speak but they can't move!'

'Don't worry, I've got an idea,' said Peanut. 'Can you guys hold Alan there for a second?'

'We'll try,' yelled Dad.

Peanut ran over to the paintings that Mr White had stolen, grabbed the *Mona Lisa* and carefully prised it from its thick, wooden frame. She then ran back and, with Mum's help, wedged the chunky rectangle over Alan's head and shoulders. It was a tight squeeze, but it worked. Alan was completely trapped. There was no way he was escaping now.

67's Master

'7! WHERE'S NERYS?' shouted an out-of-breath Peanut. 'WHAT HAVE YOU DONE WITH HER?'

'Nerys? Who is Nerys?' replied the incapacitated robot. 'Oh, you mean the miniscule Welsh human that I extracted from the lake earlier?'

'You know exactly who I'm talking about,' said Peanut, sharply.

'And why, Medium-sized Human, are you so interested in the whereabouts of Miniscule Welsh Human?'

'Just tell us where she is!' demanded Peanut. She could feel her heart beating faster as the anger rose.

'Ah, I think that I might know why you are so desperate to find her,' said 67, slyly.

Peanut shot a nervous look to her dad.

'It's because she has Pencil Number One, correct?' said 67.

Peanut went white.

'Oh yes, Peanut Jones, I know all about the pencil. I assume you are worried that Miniscule Welsh Human might have given me Conté's prototype?' continued the RAZER.

'67, this is your final warning. Tell us where Nerys is right now,' Dad said quietly.

'Do not worry, Gary Jones,' said 67. 'She is perfectly safe. And fret not, Peanut Jones, she still has the pencil. I can promise you that.'

'Either tell us where Nerys is RIGHT NOW,' said Dad, his voice rising menacingly, 'or I will personally make sure that you experience the shortest circuit in the history of robotics. Your restraining bolts, bad motivators and, er, flux capacitors will wish they had never been soldered together in the first place!'

'Your scientifically inaccurate threats do not frighten me, Gary Jones,' said 67. 'Do you really think it matters what you do with *me*? Because, newsflash: it really doesn't. Not one quark. I am but a machine, built to serve my master, and I have already fulfilled my purpose. The plan has played out perfectly. Every step of the way, you humans have all done exactly what we wanted you to, blindly doing our bidding at every single turn.'

'*Our* bidding?' said Leo, confused. 'Your *master*? Are you talking about Alan? Has Josephine's little device-thingy knocked out your vision or something? Because, *newsflash*, we have just captured the big lummox! He's sitting right here with an ornate picture frame around him!'

At this, the robot began to make a strange, unfamiliar noise. It sounded like . . . giggling.

'Er, what are you doing?' said Leo.

'*Ha ha ha ha ha ha HA HA HA HA!*' 67's giggling quickly grew into a full-on belly laugh.

Up until this point in their lives, none of them had ever heard a robot emit so much as a chuckle before, let alone a guffaw as hearty as the one coming from 67. It was a truly strange, and slightly bone-chilling, sound.

'What's so funny?' said Peanut.

'I'll tell you what's so funny, Peanut Jones,' replied the RAZER between cackles. 'The idea that this knucklehead was ever *important*. The idea that this walking hunk of meat was ever anything more than necessary muscle.'

Alan frowned at the robot, an even more confused expression on his face than usual.

'Was Alan my master? HA! HA! HA!' said the howling 67.

'Hang on,' said Alan, flexing his bulging arms, which made the wooden frame creak. 'What do you mean I was nothing more than necessary muscle?'

'It's not really that hard to understand, Knuckle-headed Human,' replied the chortling robot. 'Even for a below-average thinker like you.'

'But . . . but . . . you told me that I would be given an important role,' said Alan quietly. 'That I would have my own office and everything. With a coffee machine, one of those little jellybean dispensers and a metal ball clinky-clanky swinging toy thing.'

'You see?' said the robot to Peanut between snickers. 'A total meathead. He has been played just as much as the rest of you have. I've said it before and I'll say it again, humankind really is a very basic species. Very basic indeed.'

Alan slumped to the floor, shaking his head. Dad and Leo released their grip slightly, and Peanut found herself feeling a little bit sorry for him.

'So, who *have* you been working with then?' Peanut asked 67. 'Whose plan was it? Who *is* your master?'

'Why, the same person that it has always been,' replied the robot. 'Mr White, of course.'

'Again, I'm not sure if something's happened to your microcontrollers,' said Rockwell. 'But Mr White is currently knee-deep in plaster in the Rainbow Lake, being guarded by two superheroes and feeling very sorry for himself. I've just seen him with my own eyes.'

'Are you sure about that, Tall Human?' said 67, ominously.

'*HELP ME! HELP ME, PLEASE!*'

The cry came from beneath the hatch in front of the desk. The one that had once led to the swimming pool full of rainbow-coloured water.

'Nerys?' whispered Mum. 'That sounds like Nerys!'

She ran over and pulled open the wooden door.

'TRACEY? PLEASE! *HELP ME!* I'M SCARED!' said Nerys from inside, her voice louder now that the hatch was open.

'SHE'S IN HERE!' shouted Mum to the others. 'Come on, we have to rescue her!'

Wasting no time, she went straight down the hatch, closely followed by Dad, Leo and Doodle.

'DON'T WORRY, NERYS,' Tracey yelled, her voice echoing around the now-empty pool room. 'WE'RE HERE NOW! EVERYTHING'S GOING TO BE ALL RIGHT!'

50
The Truth

As Mum, Dad, Leo and Doodle disappeared through the hatch, something caught Peanut's eye. It was *The Scream*, Edvard Munch's 1893 masterpiece in oils, leaning against the wall. Mr White had stolen it from the National Gallery in Oslo several months earlier.

And then it began.

Slowly, silently, a figure emerged from behind the painting. They were wearing a suit, shirt and tie so white that they appeared to be made of actual light. On top of their head was a similarly dazzling fedora, pulled down low over their eyes. The agonised face in Munch's painting was a perfect reflection of the children's feelings in that moment.

'M-M-Mr White?' stammered Rockwell. 'B-b-but you're

stuck in plaster down in the lake. You're . . . you're . . .
Mr Stone. I-I-I just saw you!'

The gleaming figure carefully put down the walkie-talkie
they were holding and then, with a surprising burst of speed
and purpose, reached into their jacket pocket.

Peanut, sensing danger, pulled the spray can from her
bandolier as fast as she could and aimed it at the figure.
But she was too slow. White was the faster gunslinger.

By the time Peanut's finger had found the button on the
can's nozzle, White had already taken Little Tail from their
pocket and, with a flick of a wrist, used the eraser to rub out a
tiny section of an almost-invisible graphite line that stretched
from the floor to the highest point of the ceiling. Instantly,
a large pencil-drawn cage plummeted to the ground, trapping
the helpless Peanut, Little-Bit and Rockwell.

'HA!' shouted a gleeful 67. 'It has happened again!
We managed to get you humans right where we wanted you!
You were standing in exactly the right place! Honestly, this is
far too easy.'

Not missing a beat, White rushed over to the hatch in the
floor and slid the cast-iron bolt across, locking it. Then they
turned to face the caged children and smiled.

The room was silent for a good ten seconds, before a
shell-shocked Peanut eventually spoke.

'I . . . I don't understand,' she said to White, her voice

shaking and confused. 'If . . . if . . . if you're *not* Mr Stone, then . . . who *are* you?'

White tucked the pencil back into their inside jacket pocket, raised a gloved hand and pushed back the brim of the fedora. Then they tilted their face upwards towards the light and looked directly at Peanut. Eventually, they said the two words that revealed the truth – a truth that, unbeknownst to her, had been staring Peanut in the face for a very long time.

'Hiya, lovely.'

51
Snakes

'Nerys!? *Y-you're* Mr White?'

Even though she could hear the words coming out of her own mouth, Peanut couldn't quite believe what she was saying.

'That's right, lovely,' replied Nerys, smiling. 'Oh dear, has it come as a bit of a shock?'

'But . . . but . . . you've always been so . . . *nice.*'

'A means to an end, I'm afraid,' said Nerys. 'I have found, over the years, that a certain . . . veneer of amiability has been necessary to help me accomplish my goals.' Her upbeat, lilting Welsh accent suddenly seemed less sunny than it had done before. More . . . creepy. It sent a chill down Peanut's spine.

'But . . . what about all that stuff about Mr Stone in

Milan? You said he kept talking about the heir,' said a confused Rockwell.

'And that he had threatened you and Mum!' cried Peanut.

'And when 67 and his RAZERs took you hostage in the Rainbow Lake,' added Little-Bit, 'you looked so scared!'

'You're right, little one,' said Nerys. 'I did, didn't I? I'm not gonna lie, it turns out that I'm quite the actor! I was particularly proud of that anguished *HEEEELLLLP MEEEEEE!* as the robots lifted me from the lake. And what about that little turn just now, through the walkie-talkie? *TRACEY? PLEASE! HELP ME! I'M SCARED!* An impressive bit of work, if I do say so myself.'

'But . . . Mr Stone . . . he wears the same hat as Mr White . . .' said Peanut, still struggling to get her head around what was happening.

'Yes,' replied Nerys. 'That's because *I* bought it for him. A little present from an appreciative staff member. I told him that it offset his black suit beautifully and made his eyes pop. He really is quite suggestable, you know. Most weak-minded men are, I find. And guess what, we have the same hat size! Isn't that a happy coincidence?'

The children stood in stunned silence.

'And I'll tell you what else makes me happy,' continued Nerys. 'The fact that you're all neatly squirrelled away in that cage. Don't worry, though, because the good news is that you'll have a great view as I carry out the final part of my little plan.'

'Not *everyone* is in the cage, lassie!' said a gruff voice. 'I think you've forgotten about little ol' me.'

It was Woodhouse! He emerged from behind the desk, his long tail curling and winding behind him threateningly.

'I think it's time you and I had a wee chat,' he said. 'It seems you've been causing my pals here a spot of bother.'

'Oh dear,' said Nerys, calmly. 'A rat. You know, I've always hated rodents. They really are the lowest of the low. I mean, what are they actually *for*? Oh well, I suppose we'll just have to sort you out, won't we? Let's see . . .'

She pulled Little Tail from her jacket pocket and started to draw long, swooping lines in the air. Ten seconds later, she was done.

The illustrated snake landed on the floor in a slippery coil, before rearing up and directing its serpentine gaze straight at Woodhouse.

'P-p-p-python,' said the terrified rat, his eyes as wide as saucers.

The snake's forked tongue flickered in its mouth, and a huge smile began to creep across its scaly face.

'I think my friend here is a bit peckish,' said Nerys, whose voice sounded more like Mr White's by the second. 'Why don't you grab yourself some lunch, Monty?'

Suddenly, the snake sprang towards Woodhouse at a frightening speed. The rat, displaying a pretty impressive turn of pace of his own, leapt from the desk and ran for his life. The three caged children shrieked, afraid for their friend.

Rockwell, who had apparently got over his phobia of rats, yelled, 'Run, Woodhouse, run!'

'I'll be back,' Woodhouse shouted over his shoulder before disappearing into the corridor, with the illustrated snake in hot pursuit.

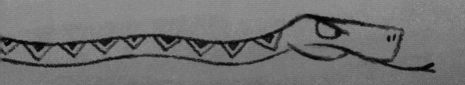

Peanut turned to Nerys. 'You monster!' she seethed.

Nerys smiled. 'Sorry about that, lovelies,' she said, cheerily. 'Just a little bit of pest control. Right, where were we? Ah yes, the final part of my plan.'

Nerys snapped her fingers and twelve gold RAZERs instantly glided into the room, arranging themselves in a V formation behind her. Their eyes were glowing bright red, unlike the purple swirls that 67 and 72 still displayed. Nerys brought Little Tail up to her eye and took a long, hard look at its sharp point.

'Righty-ho,' she said, cheerily. 'Let's get rid of all this creativity nonsense once and for all, shall we?'

52
The Trigger

'old RAZER 003, set that big oaf free, would you?' barked Nerys.

The robot sped over to Alan, produced a tiny circular saw from its side panel and cut through the *Mona Lisa*'s frame. It fell to the floor in two pieces. 003 then cut through the tape binding his arms and legs. Once free, Alan stretched his arms out to the sides and wiggled his thick fingers. But he thanked neither the robot nor Nerys.

'There's still something I don't understand,' said Rockwell. 'And that's—'

'Oh, trust me, there's a lot you don't understand, Tall Human,' said 67 gleefully, eyes still purple and swirling.

'Yes, well, fortunately, Rockwell, it doesn't matter

whether you understand or not,' said Nerys. 'All three of you have been an enormous help without even knowing it. As have your mother and that poor, ridiculous man, Mr Stone. I suppose all those years spent pretending to work for them weren't totally wasted, after all.'

'I have a question,' said Peanut, quietly.

'Go on then, lovely. Ask away.'

'Why?'

'Why, what?' replied Nerys.

'Why all this? Why do you want to rid the world of its creativity? There must be a reason. I mean, why do you hate art so much?'

Nerys smiled, shook her head, and walked over to the chair next to the control desk.

'You might find this hard to believe, young Peanut,' she said as she sat down, 'but I was a very artistic child. Full disclosure: I didn't enjoy school, and school didn't enjoy me. But the one thing I was good at was art. In fact, the only time that people would notice me was when I drew or painted. I was invisible until I picked up a pencil. My classmates only ever wanted to be friends with me for the duration of the art lesson though. After that, everything would go back to normal and I'd be on my own again. But at least I had the art room. I loved that place. It was somewhere I could retreat to whenever I felt lonely. The pictures that I made there were my friends, and they never stole my lunch money or laughed at me behind my back.'

'Well, in that case, this makes *no* sense at all,' said Little-Bit. 'If you love art, why are you trying to destroy it?'

'My parents never understood,' continued Nerys, ignoring the question. 'They didn't view art as a worthwhile subject to study at school, let alone something that a person could ever make a *career* out of. "A waste of time", they called it.'

'What a load of rubbish,' said Peanut.

'That's what I thought at the time too,' said Nerys. 'And I hated them for saying it. Then they made me leave school at the age of fifteen and forced me to take a typing position at a local accountancy firm. "A proper job", they called it.'

'Sounds pretty boring to me,' said Little-Bit.

'It *was* boring. So I carried on with my art regardless,' continued Nerys. 'I would paint in my bedroom whenever I could and take myself off to art galleries and life-drawing classes at every opportunity. Then, when I turned eighteen,

I secretly applied to go to the Royal College of Art. It was a lifelong dream of mine. Unfortunately for me, competition was high and I was told that I wouldn't be offered a place.'

'Why not?' asked Rockwell. 'Were you rubbish?'

'I certainly was not!' shouted Nerys, with venom in her eyes. 'If you must know, they said my style was too naïve and that I didn't have a solid enough grasp of the foundations. *Pah!* What nonsense! I think perhaps being a female applicant in the 1960s had much more to do with it. I bet there were loads of men – with less talent – who were offered places.'

'So, what happened next?' asked Peanut.

'Well, I was furious, obviously,' she said. 'Furious with the art college for rejecting me, furious with my parents for not encouraging my creativity when I was younger, and furious with the world for not providing me with the opportunities that I deserved!'

Peanut looked at Nerys's hands. They were shaking.

'I remember leaving the interview and just walking around London in a daze. I must have gone all the way from Kensington to Soho, because I suddenly found myself stood on the Charing Cross Road right outside the National Portrait Gallery. Galleries had always been my happy place, so I decided to go inside and try to cheer myself up. That's when I found it.'

'Found what?' asked Peanut, already knowing the answer.

'That's when I found the door.'

NATIONAL PORTRAIT GALLERY

53
Nerys in Chroma

'It was hidden behind a plinth holding a bust of Queen Victoria,' said Nerys, quietly. 'I don't know what drew me to it, but something did. When I saw the door, I just knew that I had to go through.'

She stood up and walked over to the drawings of doors on the wall behind the control desk.

'Ah, Chroma,' she said. 'What a place. From the moment I walked down that leafy passageway and into the Green Valleys for the first time, I just knew that I belonged here. The views, the colours, the sounds. It felt like I'd finally come home.'

'That's exactly how I felt too,' said Peanut. 'The difference is that I didn't decide to dedicate my whole life to finding a way to destroy it.'

Nerys ignored her and continued, a wistful look in her eyes. 'I soon found out that Chroma was the source of *all* the world's creative energy, and that all of the great artists throughout history had visited at some point to swim in the Rainbow Lake. I think the first person I met told me that! It made me love the place even more.'

'Hang on,' said Rockwell. 'If you knew that, why didn't you just dive into the lake, have a little swim about and then go back home having become a much better artist? Just like Dalí and van Gogh did? You'd have probably got a place at art college straight away.'

'I'm sure I would have,' she replied. 'But, unfortunately, I can't swim. My parents didn't ever take me to lessons. One more way in which they failed me.'

Peanut nodded, remembering her dad dragging Nerys through the water after they'd all been pushed into the lake earlier that day.

'So you decided to move here instead?' asked Little-Bit.

'Initially, I thought I'd just hang around until teatime. But a week passed before I knew it! At that point, I figured that I should probably head back home. I knew I might get into terrible trouble with my parents for being away for so long, but I didn't care. *So what* if they'd been worried sick? That being said, you can imagine my surprise when I discovered that, as far as they were concerned, I'd only been gone for a

few hours. As you now know, time moves at different speeds across the dimensions. This whole Chroma thing just got better and better!'

'So, when did it all change?' asked Rockwell. 'When did you decide that you needed to destroy it?'

'That very night, actually,' replied Nerys. 'On the train back to Wales, it occurred to me that if there had been fewer creative people who wanted to go to the Royal College of Art, then I might have got a place there after all. Then it hit me. If Chroma was the source of all the world's creativity, all I had to do was put a stop to that and then I'd have no more competition.'

She pulled Little Tail from her pocket.

'So, I began to draw up my masterplan,' she said. Her Welsh accent had now totally disappeared, and she sounded exactly like Mr White had the first time they had met him on the snowfields of the North Draw. 'What with the time difference between Chroma and the real world, I decided that it made sense to play the long game. And, boy, has it been a *long* game! Over many years, I'd visit the city regularly, staying for weeks at a time. I learned about all its stories and legends – including that of Pencil Number One and Conté's heir – its history and its political structure. I got to know the system inside out, and after a year or two I'd formulated a plan. I decided to run for mayor. If I could get control of the city, that's when I could begin to shut it down as a creative force.'

'I hate to say this,' said Rockwell, 'but as a plan, that's actually pretty solid. Albeit in an incredibly selfish and evil way.'

'I knew that I, Nerys, couldn't run for mayor, though,' she said. 'Those lonely years at school taught me that I didn't have the charisma to attract voters. So, I decided to invent a new persona. A character that people would warm to. Someone they would follow.'

She reached up, lifted the fedora from her head and held it out in front of her.

'And that's when I became . . . Mr White.'

54

Becoming Mr White

erys put the hat back on her head. She walked over to the wall and started to rub out the door marked *NYC* – the one that had taken Peanut, Little-Bit and Rockwell to New York on their last visit. Peanut winced.

'Why did you decide to call yourself Mr White?' asked Little-Bit from the cage. 'Why not something more . . . imaginative?'

'Yeah,' said Rockwell, 'like Mr Partypooper or Mr Vibekill?'

'Very witty,' said Nerys, sarcastically. 'Well, if you must know, the name Nerys comes from the traditional Welsh name Generys, which means White Lady,' she replied proudly. 'So the name *White* was a no-brainer, really.'

'No-brainer is right,' scoffed Rockwell. Nerys scowled at him.

'HEY!' A muffled cry came from the hatch, followed by lots of banging. 'LET US OUT!' It was Dad.

'NERYS?' shouted Mum. 'IT DOESN'T NEED TO BE LIKE THIS. WHATEVER HAS HAPPENED, WHATEVER YOU'VE DONE, WE CAN SORT IT. JUST LET US OUT!'

'The name *White* also made my outfit choice easier,' continued Nerys, totally ignoring the voices. 'Image is important when running for office, and I wanted to stand out from the crowd. In a city that's full of colour, a white suit worked perfectly. I thought a hat would help me to keep a certain amount of anonymity, and I was obviously right – you lot had no idea who I really was!'

Peanut turned away, still annoyed at the fact that she'd been wrong about White's true identity. That's when she first noticed Alan staring at her. It was almost as if he was trying to catch her eye. It kind of creeped Peanut out.

'Wearing this costume really helped,' said Nerys as she began rubbing out the door marked M for Milan. 'I felt like a different person. Much more confident. More assertive. More powerful. All my insecurities just seemed to . . . disappear. Over the years, I gained people's trust, people of real influence in the city, like Josephine Engelberger, whose ideas about robotics immediately appealed to me. I imagined what it would be like to have an entire robot army at my beck and call. I don't suppose Nerys would ever have thought like that, and she certainly wouldn't have been able to talk all these people into following her. But Mr White had no problems whatsoever. As White, I would drop little nuggets into the conversation here and there, y'know, telling people what I would do if I were running things in Chroma. How I would colour-correct the Rainbow Lake more regularly, build more art galleries, make sure that every child was given their own set of water-soluble magic markers. All that nonsense. Everybody lapped it up.'

Peanut nodded. She could see exactly how White had gradually forced his will onto the unsuspecting public, and all it took was a few insincere promises. It was scary how easy it was for this sort of thing to happen. Horrifying, really.

At this point, Alan caught Peanut's eye again. He was staring straight at her, eyebrows raised, and he appeared to be jerking his head towards the hatch. Peanut had no idea what he was doing.

'I was *so* successful,' continued Nerys while rubbing out the Paris door, 'that by the time I announced that I was going to run for mayor, nobody was surprised. In fact, they all predicted that I'd win by a landslide. And guess what? They were right!'

'How long until they realised you were a complete and utter fraud?' spat Peanut.

Nerys smiled and moved on to the door marked B for Beijing. 'Oh, that happened very quickly, lovely. Just after I'd passed the law banning anyone from swimming in the Rainbow Lake. Or maybe it was when I'd made all artistic apparatus illegal. I don't recall. Either way, by the time they realised what was happening, it was too late. Much, much too late.'

Nerys in the Real World

erys started rubbing out one of the two remaining doors left on the wall.

'Gold RAZERs 005 and 006,' she barked, 'get Peanut Jones out of the cage and bring her to me. I need to show her something. Oh, and make sure she's restrained.'

Two robots whizzed over to the cage. One unlocked the cell door, wrapped their extendable metal arms around Peanut and pulled her out, while the other relocked the door behind them. Rockwell and Little-Bit both tried to grab Peanut's hand, but it was no use. The RAZERs moved too quickly.

As they zoomed past with Peanut, Alan had to jump

behind the control desk, otherwise they would have knocked him over. Again, he caught the girl's eye, his eyebrows raised. A curious notion suddenly entered her head. Maybe Alan was trying to tell her something. Could he be trying to . . . *help them*?! He had been well and truly done over by Nerys, after all.

'Tidy,' said Nerys once the RAZERs were next to her.

'OK,' said Peanut, shooting a curious glance at Alan. 'Shall I ask the obvious question? Why are you rubbing out these doors?'

'Two reasons,' replied Nerys. 'First, I have no need for these portals anymore. And second, because I need to make room for the big one that I'm about to draw.'

'Why are you drawing a new one?'

'You'll see,' said Nerys as she erased the final hinge on the final door. 'By the way, would you like to hear about the beautiful coincidence in this whole fascinating story? It really is quite incredible.'

'Not really,' said Peanut. 'But I'm sure you're going to tell me anyway.'

'Yes, lovely, I am. When I wasn't running for high office in Chroma, I was spending my time in the real world working admin jobs at various boring accountancy firms. I needed to earn a bit of money after all.'

As she spoke, she started to draw a huge arch on the wall with Little Tail.

'I ended up in London,' continued Nerys, 'at a very whizz-bang firm called – you've guessed it – Blood, Stone & Partners. The work was as dull as ever, but at least the offices were pretty close to the National Portrait Gallery. Handy for my regular trips to Chroma. I had been elected mayor by this point and my masterplan was well under way.'

'And that's when you met Mum,' said Peanut.

'Indeed,' said Nerys. 'I was working for one of the directors, a slimy toad of a man called Stone who was habitually rude to everybody. So I was relieved when your mum joined and I was asked to be her assistant too. It made my annoying job slightly less annoying.'

'Mum always talked fondly about you,' said Peanut sadly. 'How could you be so two-faced?'

'Ha!' said Nerys. 'Literally! I have two faces, Nerys's and Mr White's. Your mum is a nice lady, I must admit. Although she did have a tendency to bang on about her home life.'

A loud sobbing sound came from the hatch in the floor where Mum, Dad, Leo and Doodle were trapped. It sounded like Mum.

'I can't tell you how many times I heard how proud she was of her children,' continued Nerys. 'Or how lovely her husband was. It was just so much *blah blah blah*.'

Peanut and Little-Bit looked at each other and shared a small smile. Alan, meanwhile, subtly edged a few centimetres closer to the hatch.

'One of her saving graces, however,' continued Nerys, 'was the fact that her husband was a failing artist. He didn't seem to be able to sell any of his paintings. As you can imagine, this filled me with happiness. I'd pretend to be all sympathetic when Tracey was telling me how worried she was, but inside I always danced a little celebratory jig. I love hearing about other people not doing well. It always makes me feel better about my own . . . shortcomings.'

'And, as we know, there are plenty of those,' said Rockwell, wryly.

'Meanwhile, back in Chroma,' continued Nerys, who, by now, had almost finished drawing a wonky, but impressive, ornamented arched doorway on the wall, 'I became aware that a Resistance movement was developing. We found out that a group of citizens, led by the Markmakers, had banded together in an attempt to put a stop to my plans. Laughable,

really. But, nevertheless, it was something I kept an eye on. By this point, I had persuaded Josephine Engelberger to make me an army of robots, a shoal of flying mechanical fish, and the beginnings of a fleet of Big X vehicles that would help with the mono-ing of the city. With an army that size, I had spies everywhere. Imagine my surprise when we discovered that one of the leading operatives in the Resistance was a man called Gary Jones, and that he was married to my boss back in London! You see? A beautiful coincidence!'

'Not sure *beautiful* is the word I'd use,' said Peanut, under her breath.

'So, I decided to kill two birds with one *stone*, pardon the pun,' continued Nerys. 'Since I knew where Gary lived and had a pretty good idea of his movements, thanks to his wife's constant jabbering, I decided to take him prisoner. I waited until I knew he would be alone in the house and then despatched Alan to kidnap him and stick him in the Spire, which I had turned into a prison. For once, Alan was very effective.'

Peanut thought she saw a flash of anger cross the henchman's face.

'I personally wrote a little goodbye note, in Gary's handwriting, and instructed Alan to leave it in your house. Then I backed it up a few days later with a postcard *supposedly* sent from Gary while overseas. It was all pretty convincing, I thought.'

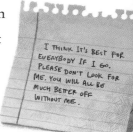

I THINK IT'S BEST FOR EVERYBODY IF I GO. PLEASE DON'T LOOK FOR ME. YOU WILL ALL BE MUCH BETTER OFF WITHOUT ME.

'Well, *I* didn't believe it,' said Peanut angrily. 'Not for one second! For a start, your handwriting was nowhere near as nice as Dad's.'

Nerys frowned. 'Of course, I then had to endure several weeks of Tracey crying about her husband leaving her to go and live in Mexico City. But it was a small price to pay to get Gary out of the picture. I even managed to sow the seed that ended up convincing your mum that all artistic pursuits in life were pointless. I was delighted when she told me that she'd moved you to St Hubert's School for the Seriously Scientific and Terminally Mathematic. It's the little victories that bring me real pleasure, you know?'

'That was your idea?!' said Peanut. 'What a truly horrible person you are.'

Nerys smiled and took a step back to admire her artwork. The new doorway was almost finished.

'Just one more thing to add,' she said, before drawing an elaborately curly door handle. 'There. All done.'

She tucked Little Tail back into her jacket pocket and turned to face Peanut, who was still in the grip of the golden RAZER.

'Right then, lovely,' Nerys said. 'Let's go back to where it all started, shall we?'

56
The Execution

erys turned the handle. The door opened onto a long, leafy passageway, at the end of which was a small wooden door, about a metre high.

'Recognise this place?' she asked Peanut as the RAZER forced her to peer through the opening.

'It's the Green Valleys portal,' said Peanut. 'The one that leads to the National Portrait Gallery.'

'Indeed,' replied the woman. 'It's also the last remaining gateway between Chroma and the real world. Well, for anyone who doesn't have a pencil like this, that is . . .' Nerys pulled Little Tail from her pocket and twirled it between her fingers like a drummer in an eighties rock band. 'I thought it would be nice for you to personally witness me getting rid of the very last portal in Chroma,' she said with a sneer in her voice.

Every instinct in Peanut's body screamed at her to reach out to grab the pencil, but her arms were pinned tightly to her side by the RAZER.

'Do you remember when we first met, lovely?' asked Nerys.

'Which one of you are we talking about? Nerys or Mr White?' asked Peanut. She was having trouble keeping track of everything and was slightly dizzy from Nerys's long story.

'Mr White, of course,' said Nerys. 'My true self. I remember our first meeting *very* clearly. It was via a video screen. I was sitting in this very room – my control room – and you were sitting in a cell just around the corner.'

'How could I forget?' Peanut rolled her eyes.

Nerys stepped through the illustrated door and started walking down the leafy passageway. The robot holding Peanut followed.

'Imagine my surprise,' continued Nerys, 'when my spies spotted *you* and your little friends making their way through the city with a small illustrated dog. Tracey and Gary Jones's annoying daughter, Pernilla!'

Peanut didn't say anything but narrowed her eyes at Nerys. The *Pernilla* thing hurt every time.

'Then, after you'd been captured, and you and I had that video call, I was trying to find out if you knew where your

father was,' continued Nerys. 'I had no idea that you were concealing something *much* more important from me.'

'You mean the pencil, don't you?' said Peanut, remembering how Alan had knocked Little Tail out of her hand, sending it flying through the window of the Spire, only for it to be returned to her by the gold-crested kaleidoscoppi.

'I do mean the pencil,' said Nerys, crouching down as they approached the end of the passageway. 'I couldn't believe it! Pencil Number One, Conté's prototype, right there in front of me! I had heard of it, of course, but I always thought it was a myth. At that moment, everything changed. Once I knew the pencil was real, I *had* to have it. I'd heard about its portal-creating powers, and I realised that if I owned the pencil I'd be able to get rid of all the other portals. Then no one but me would ever be able to travel between the two worlds!'

They'd reached the end of the passageway and were standing a few metres from the little wooden door. Nerys knelt down, and at that moment it felt to Peanut like the RAZER's grip got a little tighter.

'I had also heard about the prophecy,' Nerys said.

'And what prophecy is that?' asked Peanut, feigning ignorance.

'The one saying that if Conté's true heir holds the pencil, all of Chroma's previously lost creativity would be restored.'

'Oh,' said Peanut. '*That* prophecy.'

The Last Portal

'As luck would have it,' said Nerys as she crawled beneath the low branches to the door, 'I'd already done a lot of work to make sure your father would not get his hands on the pencil, even though I didn't yet know that the pencil existed.'

'What do you mean?' asked Peanut.

'Long before you arrived in Chroma, I was aware that the Resistance were trying to break Gary out of the Spire. So I decided to take matters into my own hands. I ordered my most trusted RAZER, 67, to pretend to go rogue and join the Resistance. Together, we decided that 67 would break your father out of jail and lead him to one of the disused cleaning stations in Modernia. That way, Gary would *think* he was free, but really, we would know exactly where he was at all times. It was perfect.'

'PERFECTLY EVIL!' shouted Gary, from the hatch.

Peanut's eyes widened as Nerys turned the pencil around and started rubbing out the Green Valleys portal. She took a deep breath and tried to compose herself. She didn't want to give Nerys the satisfaction of knowing how frightened she was. Once that portal was erased, there was no way for her and her family to ever get back home. Not without Little Tail, at least. She decided to try to keep Nerys talking.

'So if you already knew where he was,' said Peanut, 'why did you ask me about him on that video call?'

'It's called subterfuge, lovely,' Nerys sneered. 'Deception. Trickery. You should try it sometime. Anyway, when I found out that the pencil *was* real, the need to keep Gary away from it suddenly became my main priority. When I eventually got my hands on it after I stole it from you on the snowfields of the North Draw, I began to execute a new plan. The first part of this plan was to make *you* think that you knew Mr White's secret identity. I couldn't risk you guessing that he was actually me. So, I bought another hat just like mine for Mr Stone and convinced him to wear it whenever possible. It worked like a dream. I believe he turned up at your house wearing it that very evening.'

Peanut swallowed. She had to admit that she had been well and truly played by Nerys.

'The next part of the plan was to start erasing the existing portals, one by one. And it was going perfectly until you stole the pencil back from me.' She turned to face Peanut. 'That was *very* naughty of you, young lady.'

'Sorry not sorry,' she said as Nerys continued to rub out the Green Valleys portal.

Peanut turned to look back into the control room. She noticed that Alan was secretly scrabbling around on the floor, pulling at something. What was he up to now? Could he possibly be trying to open the hatch and free Leo, Doodle and her parents? That's certainly what it *looked* like he was doing.

'Anyway, I realised that if I wanted to get the pencil back, I would have to exploit your biggest weakness.'

'And what might that be?' asked Peanut, trying to buy a bit more time for whatever it was that Alan was up to.

'Why, your biggest weakness is love, of course,' said Nerys. 'I knew you wouldn't be able to resist coming to your mother's rescue if you thought Mr White had taken her hostage. That's why I persuaded Mr Stone to change the ballet reservations and take her to Milan instead of London. I knew you'd come after her. And, because I'd already made you think that Stone was White, I knew that you would try to take him, well, *us*, back to Chroma too. The whole aim, right from the moment you stole back the pencil, was to get you to *give* it back to me. Ideally when we were in Chroma. And that's exactly what you did when we were "trapped" in the Rainbow Lake.'

Nerys finished rubbing out the door. Then she turned to face Peanut and smiled. Peanut gulped.

'So, you see, lovely, everything happened this way because *I* engineered it. It was all designed and directed by *my* hand. You must admit, I am something of a genius, am I not?'

'I'll admit no such thing,' said Peanut, straining against the RAZER's gripping arms. 'So now that you've destroyed all of the portals and you've got the pencil, what do you plan to do with it?'

'Well, that's easy,' replied Nerys, smiling. 'I'm going to do what I should have done the last time I had it in my hands.'

'And what's that?' asked Peanut.

Nerys held Little Tail up in front of her face.

'I'm going to destroy it.'

Part Five

...in which Peanut arrives
at the end of the rainbow

58
The Only Creative Person in the World

'So, let's say that you do destroy Little Tail,' said Peanut, a bead of sweat appearing on her brow. 'That would mean that *nobody* would ever be able to travel between Chroma and the real world again, not now that you've rubbed out all of the existing portals.'

'I know,' said Nerys, laughing, as she walked back up the leafy passageway towards the illustrated door in the control-room wall. 'Isn't it delicious?'

'It's evil, that's what it is,' Peanut spat.

'Well, evil is a subjective concept. One woman's "evil" is another woman's . . . "innovative".'

Peanut glanced over at Alan again. He was still on his knees by the trapdoor. 'But . . . but . . . if you do destroy the pencil, *nobody*, including you, will ever be able to get back home again.'

'Well, there are certainly no flies on you, lovely,' said Nerys. 'What you are failing to grasp, however, is the fact that I am not going to do it until I am safely back in London, along with my little art collection over there by the wall. Imagine what everybody will say when I bring back all these priceless artefacts that they had thought were gone forever. I'll be quite the hero, won't I? Wouldn't be surprised if I get to meet the king.'

Peanut swallowed hard, her arms still pinned to her sides.

'But that's not the best part,' continued Nerys. 'You see, once the world loses access to Chroma, its creative hub, the number of people interested in making art will start to dwindle. They just won't feel the need to pick up a pencil, throw a pot, or paint a portrait anymore. I imagine that within a few years that compulsion for making art will have disappeared off the face of the earth, leaving little ol' me as the only creative person in the world.'

'But . . . at some point *you'll* lose the urge to be creative too,' said Peanut, still desperately playing for time.

'I'll bring my own small supply of rainbow water to dip into should I ever feel the need.' Nerys pointed to a large barrel, on top of which sat the Jinou Yonggu Cup of Emperor

Qianlong. 'Not quite the same as a swim in the Rainbow Lake, which I've never had the privilege of doing, but a cupful poured over the old noggin every now and then will certainly have an effect.'

Peanut's eyes widened. Nerys really had thought of everything. She could feel the panic rising inside her.

'So, you see,' continued Nerys. 'My skills will finally be appreciated, and I will get the recognition I deserve.'

'And what about Chroma?' asked Peanut, the colour draining from her face.

'What about it?' Nerys replied. 'I won't ever need to come back, will I? And I won't have to worry about anyone else visiting the city and swimming in the Rainbow Lake because no one will be able to get there. The portals are all gone, remember.'

Peanut looked over to Alan again. He was still on the floor, but there was no sign of Leo or her parents. *He must be struggling to open the trapdoor*, she thought to herself. She took a deep breath and, with one final effort, pushed as hard as she could against RAZER 005's metal arms. But it was no use. They didn't budge. The flame of hope flickering inside her was slowly being extinguished.

'Don't worry though, lovely,' continued Nerys. 'You can stay here for as long as you like. And when I say *as long as you like*, I mean . . . forever!'

Peanut swallowed hard. Several images flashed through her mind: her house on Melody Road, her bedroom, her dog Giles, her cat Catface, Auntie Jean, the National Portrait Gallery. She even thought of St Hubert's, the school she hated. As much as she loved the Illustrated City, the idea of never seeing any of these things again didn't bear thinking about. And also, what about Rockwell? He would miss out on so much if he were trapped in Chroma forever. For a start, he'd never get to take a maths test again! More importantly, he'd never see his mum again. At least Peanut had her whole family here. Tears began to blur her vision.

'You being trapped here would be good news for me, of course,' said Nerys. 'I wouldn't want anyone spilling the beans on how my sudden rise to prominence in the art world came about, would I?'

'Hang on. What art world?' snapped Peanut. 'There won't *be* an art world! If there's no Chroma, there is no creativity anywhere. Full stop. That means no one will care about seeing any art! Who do you think is going to be appreciating your talents, exactly?'

Nerys stopped walking and a small wrinkle

appeared between her eyebrows. She looked at Peanut as if this was something she hadn't considered until this moment.

'What's wrong?' said Peanut. 'Had that not occurred to you? Have I pointed out a slight flaw in your *masterplan*?'

Nerys stared at her blankly for a good few seconds. Then she shook her head, smiled and climbed back through the illustrated door into the control room.

'Right then, lovely,' she said, walking over to the stolen artworks by the wall. 'Enough of this nonsense. I don't see the need to delay things any longer. I'll just collect my bits and pieces and then I'll be on my way. Try not to get too upset when we say our goodbyes.'

Peanut looked over at Alan as RAZER 005 carried her through the door. The huge-shouldered man was standing up now, staring straight back at her. He nodded, ever so slightly. Peanut turned to look at Rockwell and Little-Bit in the cage. They both nodded too.

Something was going on. Peanut didn't know what exactly, but there was definitely . . . something. She felt a fluttering sensation in her tummy.

The flickering flame of hope was reignited.

59

The Cavalry

uddenly, the hatch in the floor that led to where Dad, Mum, Leo and Doodle were trapped flew open. This was the first of three unexpected events that took place in a very short space of time.

The second involved Alan smashing his massive fist into the door of the illustrated cage that was holding Rockwell and Little-Bit. It instantly broke open, freeing them both. Peanut blinked. *Did Alan really just rescue her sister and her best friend?*

Thirdly, the huge henchman dove underneath the chair and grabbed the brassy RAZER-disabling device that Rockwell had dropped. He pressed the button, turning the eyes of the gold robots in the room purple and swirly. Now paralysed, 005's metallic arms slackened, allowing Peanut to wriggle free.

A second later, Dad, Mum, Leo and Doodle came running up out of the hatch.

'Where is she?' yelled Dad, holding a walkie-talkie in his hand. 'Where's Mr Wh— er, I mean, Nerys? We heard everything she said through the walkie-talkie!'

'There she is,' shouted Little-Bit. 'Over in the corner, next to Monet's *Water Lilies!*'

'How *could* you, Nerys?' asked Mum, her face streaked with tears. 'I thought we were friends!'

'ALAN!' shouted Nerys, completely ignoring the Joneses. 'WHAT ON EARTH ARE YOU DOING?'

'Yes, Alan,' chimed the still incapacitated 67, 'please state your reason for liberating the enemy.'

'Oh, don't worry about it,' he replied. 'I'm just being a *big oaf*, as usual. I guess I just accidentally freed your prisoners with my big, meaty hands.'

'TRAITOR!' Nerys bellowed.

'No, no, no,' Alan said with a grin. 'I'm no traitor. I'm just the *necessary muscle*. And I should have stood up to you a long time ago.' His freckles had turned an angry shade of purple. 'I can't believe I ever let you talk me into being your henchman. I was perfectly happy working in that coffee shop back in The Grid. None of the other baristas *ever* called me a meathead.'

Even Alan is on our side now, Peanut thought, hardly believing it could be true. She didn't have much time to let this sink in, as Nerys picked up what priceless artefacts she could and began to make a run for it.

'LEO!' shouted Dad. 'GET HER!'

The boy made a grab for the woman as she ran towards a narrow staircase that spiralled up the tapered walls of the conical room, but he missed. Seconds later, Nerys was scrambling up the stairs with the frameless *Mona Lisa*, the Jinou Yonggu Cup of Emperor Qianlong and Little Tail in her hands. Leo, in hot pursuit, got to the first step quickly, but was immediately knocked over by the cup as it came flying down the steps. Apparently, the beautifully jewelled, solid gold work of art had been reduced to a mere missile by Nerys in order to help her escape.

'Are you all right, Leo?' asked Peanut, crouching down next to her fallen brother at the bottom of the staircase. Little-Bit and Rockwell were trying to help him up onto his feet.

'Don't worry about me, guys,' he replied, clutching his ankle in pain. 'Just go and get *her*!'

Nerys was, by now, halfway up the stairs and heading to a small door at the top marked 'Mooring Mast'.

'Leo's right!' shouted Dad as he ran towards them. 'Go, Peanut! Whatever you do, don't let her escape with that pencil!'

60
Spiders

eanut dashed up the staircase after Nerys. Little-Bit and Rockwell followed closely behind. The three of them had, by now, become a super team who worked together brilliantly, instinctively knowing what role each of them should play. Also, they had some experience of being stuck at the top of a very tall building with nothing but art supplies to help them, and, up until this point, they'd always managed to get back to down to earth safely. They couldn't risk Nerys doing the same, however.

'Peanut!' Little-Bit shouted up to her. 'Use your art equipment!'

My art equipment? thought Peanut as she bounded up the stairway, taking the steps two at a time. *Of course!* She'd totally forgotten that she was still wearing her bandolier. Its contents appeared to be in working order, despite RAZER 005's iron grip on her earlier.

She pulled the spray can from its slot, put her finger on the nozzle and aimed it at Nerys. A powerful jet of black paint flew across the void, hitting the woman on the shoulder and painting a strong black line diagonally across her back. She stopped immediately and turned to face Peanut.

'You'll have to do better than that, lovely,' Nerys said with a grin, before pulling Little Tail from her pocket and drawing several small, spiky shapes on the step below her.

'What's she drawn?' yelled Little-Bit.

'Not sure,' shouted Peanut over her shoulder. 'They look a bit like—'

'SPIDERS!' screeched Rockwell.

Sure enough, as the children got closer, it became clear that the little spiky shapes were alive. Not only that, but  they seemed to be growing bigger very quickly . . .

and they were multiplying! Soon, hundreds of huge hairy illustrated arachnids were scuttling down the stairs towards them.

'What do I do now!?' asked Peanut desperately, as the army of illustrated spiders approached. 'I'm not a huge fan of creepy-crawlies!'

'LEMONS!' shouted Rockwell.

'What?' asked Peanut.

'LEMONS!' said the boy for a second time. 'QUICK! PAINT SOME LEMONS!'

'Why?'

'JUST DO IT!' he yelled.

Peanut snatched the watercolour set from her bandolier, picked up the brush, dipped it in yellow, and began to paint three lemons in the air in front of her.

'Why am I painting lemons, Rockwell!?' she shouted down the staircase.

'Spiders hate citrus smells,' he replied, his voice getting higher as the creatures got closer. 'Cut the lemons in half and squeeze them all over the stairs in front of you!'

Peanut drew a simple knife with one of her marker pens, picked it up and sliced the fruit. Thankfully, the lemons she'd painted were very juicy, and, for once, actually smelled like they should. She squeezed them all over the steps seconds before the torrent of spiders got there. The creatures at the front of the pack stopped instantly in their tracks, causing those behind to crash into them. A huge eight-legged pile-up ensued. Then, every single one of the spiders turned around and scurried away back up the stairs.

'Yes!' Rockwell exclaimed. Little-Bit high-fived him.

'Great thinking, Rockwell!' shouted Peanut.

Nerys, meanwhile, had been busy with the pencil again. She had drawn what appeared to be a black cloud, which she now held in her hands. She turned around, brought it up to her face and blew. Slowly, it began to float across the room, getting bigger as it moved. A few seconds later, the cloud had filled up the entire top of the room, enveloping the whole staircase and the door above Peanut, Little-Bit and Rockwell.

Then the storm began.

61
The Storm

Lightning lit up the entire room for a fraction of a second, and then the ear-splitting sound of thunder rolled around the conical walls. It was louder than anything Peanut, Rockwell and Little-Bit had ever heard in their lives.

'Ow!' shouted Little-Bit. 'My ears are ringing!'

'It's because we're so close to it,' shouted Rockwell. 'We need to keep going and climb through the cloud before . . .'

He didn't finish his sentence. A huge bolt of lightning

shot through the air, missing them by no more than a couple of metres. It was accompanied by another deafening cracking noise that sounded like a bomb going off.

'Oh no,' shouted Rockwell. 'We're in the centre of the storm! We need to hurry!'

'I want to go back down, Peanut,' said Little-Bit. 'I'm scared!'

'I'm afraid we can't, LB,' said Peanut. 'We have to keep going. Everyone is counting on us. I know you're scared, but take my hand. We can do this together.'

They continued running up the stairs as the rain began to fall in huge, black, inky drops. A violent headwind began to whip around them, slowing their climb. Suddenly, another bright fork of electricity split the room, and the deafening noise that came with it nearly toppled Peanut off the edge of the staircase. Luckily, Rockwell was there to grab her arm and stop her from falling.

'Maybe LB's right,' shouted Peanut as Rockwell hauled her back onto the staircase. Her face was white. 'It's too dangerous. Maybe we should go back down!'

Rockwell frowned.

Little-Bit turned to look at him. She recognised his brainwave face and smiled. He smiled back.

'Are you thinking what I'm thinking?' he asked.

'Let's make a lightning conductor,' she replied.

'Yes!' said Rockwell. 'Pass me a pen.'

As quickly as he could, Rockwell drew a long, straight line with a small ball at its tip. He then drew another line perpendicular to the first, making an enormous and unwieldy L shape.

'Right, we need to attach this to the wall!'

All three of them moved the drawing into position so that it stuck out from the wall and extended horizontally over the void below them. The end with the ball at the top pointed straight up at the dark cloud above them.

'Brilliant, Rocky,' said an ink-streaked Little-Bit. 'Hopefully that'll intercept the next lightning bolt and channel all of that voltage into the walls of the Spire and safely down into the ground.'

'I still think that maybe we should go back down,' Peanut said, unconvinced.

'Don't give up now, Peanut!' shouted somebody just behind them.

It was Dad! He had caught up with them, along with Mum and a limping Leo.

'Listen! We have a chance to put an end to this whole thing, once and for all,' he yelled as the wind blew his curly, red hair straight. 'We *must* stop Nerys! The whole world is depending on us! Creativity is depending on us!'

'But . . . the lightning . . .' shouted Peanut. 'It's too much . . .'

'You have weathered bigger storms than this one, my little artist,' Dad said, smiling. 'I know all about your adventures in Chroma, Peanut. You're the bravest one out of all of us. If anyone can do this, it's you. Come on! One more push! One last adventure! And this time, we'll be right there with you.'

CRACK! Another lightning bolt flew from the cloud, but this time it hit the conductor, which instantly fizzed with energy. The whole group watched as the electricity travelled along Rockwell's drawing and disappeared harmlessly into the wall.

'It worked!' shouted LB. 'Rocky, it worked! Go science!'

'Brilliant, Rockwell,' shouted Dad. 'Just brilliant!'

Peanut smiled. She could feel her courage returning.

She wiped the black, inky rain from her face and remembered everything her dad had been through to get to this point. She thought about the sacrifices he'd made. Then she looked at the faces of all her favourite people: Dad, Mum, Little-Bit, Leo and Rockwell. Nerys had said that love was her greatest weakness, but she'd been wrong. Love was Peanut's greatest strength.

'You're right, Dad,' she said. 'Let's finish this . . . together!'

62
The Top of the Spire

Peanut charged up the stairs, leading the group straight into the pencil-drawn storm cloud. The inside was illuminated by flashing pockets of bright, crackling electricity, but the group managed to dodge the lightning and, to everyone's relief, arrive at the top unscathed.

Peanut looked at the door at the end of the staircase. It was just a few steps away now and it was wide open.

'Nerys must have gone through already,' she said to her ink-covered, wind-blown family. 'I just hope we're not too late.'

Peanut started to walk towards the door.

'Wait for me,' said Dad. 'I am Conté's heir, so I really

should be there with you. It's me who needs to get hold of Little Tail, after all, if the prophecy is to be fulfilled.'

Peanut grabbed her dad's hand, and then they stepped through the door together. It led to an open-air walkway no more than a metre wide, with a barrier that came up to Peanut's chest. The path completely circled the outside of the Spire a few metres below its tip. Sitting on top of that tip was a thin, white, pylon-like structure, reminiscent of the Eiffel Tower, that reached a further ten metres into the bright Chroma sky.

'Is that the mooring mast?' asked Peanut.

'I think so,' replied Dad.

'What *is* a mooring mast?' said Rockwell, as he came through the door onto the walkway with the others.

'It must be where they park the Giant X,' said Dad, as he continued to walk around. 'An airship like that would have to be tied to something when it was refuelled so that it didn't float away. Maybe that's why they added this mast to the Spire.'

Little-Bit stood on her tiptoes and looked down over the edge of the barrier.

'LB!' shouted Mum. 'Get away from the edge!'

'Look!' Little-Bit shouted. 'Superheroes! They're everywhere!'

Peanut looked over the barrier. Her sister was right! The sky below them was full of cloaked figures, criss-crossing and zig-zagging through the air.

'Wow!' she exclaimed. 'They must have escaped from the lake!'

'And if *they've* escaped, then maybe they're helping everybody else to escape too,' said Rockwell, excitedly.

'Yes! The lake looks like it's emptying of people,' said Mum.

'And that's not all,' added Leo. 'Look over there. In the snow!'

On the white expanse of the North Draw's snowfields, a dark shape was sprawled across the ground. Even from a great height, it looked huge.

'It's the Giant X!' shouted Rockwell. 'And it looks like it's been deflated! Josephine must have brought it down, just like she said she would. I bet she found a way to override 67's protocol! I mean, *of course* she did! If she can build something that disables RAZERs with the click of a button, she can definitely figure out how to do the same with Giant Xs! Gosh, she's brilliant.'

'Never mind that now,' said Dad, urgently. 'Let's stay focused. It's Nerys we're after, remember. I've just done a full circuit of the walkway and all I could find was this.' He held up the *Mona Lisa*. 'She must have dropped it. But Nerys herself is nowhere to be seen. It's like she's vanished into thin air. I've got a terrible feeling that she's already drawn a portal and left . . .'

'Er, Dad,' said Peanut. 'She hasn't left.'

'Where is she, then?' he asked.

Peanut pointed to the mast.

'She's up there.'

63

The Heir and the Pencil

Nerys was several metres above them, climbing the ladder housed inside the framework of the mooring mast. She was holding something large and black. It looked like a slightly wonky drawing of a jetpack.

'What's she doing?' asked Rockwell.

'I'm guessing she tried to draw a jetpack, like the ones I drew for us on top of the Empire State Building in New York,' said Peanut. 'But it looks like she couldn't quite get it right.'

'Ha!' laughed Rockwell. 'Typical. All the gear, no idea! Just cos you have the world's best pencil, it doesn't mean that you know how to use it!'

Little-Bit and Peanut giggled too, and the children's laughter drifted up to Nerys's ears.

'That's utter rubbish!' she shouted from high above them. She was almost at the top of the ladder now, just below the tip of the mast. 'If you must know, I, er, decided that drawing a door would be a much easier way for me to get out of here! And, as we all know, I am great at drawing doors!'

Nerys leaned back against the framework and dropped her useless jetpack illustration. They all watched as it caught the breeze and tumbled down through the sky, disappearing into the thin clouds that surrounded the Spire. Mum let out a little squeal. Peanut gulped. They were all suddenly very aware of the fact that they were *really* high up!

While most of the group was distracted by the falling jetpack, Nerys pulled Little Tail from her pocket and started to draw.

Dad, however, was keeping a close eye on her and immediately leapt into action, determined to grab the pencil. He scrambled up the steps that led to the mast and began to climb the ladder as fast as he could. Peanut followed close behind, despite Mum's loud protests.

Nerys looked down at the two Joneses as they climbed up towards her, and she began to draw in super-speed mode.

The door frame . . . the door . . .

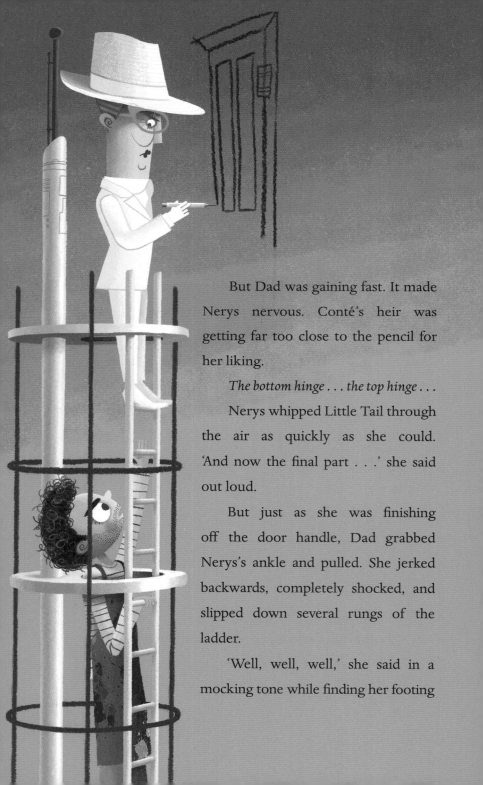

But Dad was gaining fast. It made Nerys nervous. Conté's heir was getting far too close to the pencil for her liking.

The bottom hinge . . . the top hinge . . .

Nerys whipped Little Tail through the air as quickly as she could. 'And now the final part . . .' she said out loud.

But just as she was finishing off the door handle, Dad grabbed Nerys's ankle and pulled. She jerked backwards, completely shocked, and slipped down several rungs of the ladder.

'Well, well, well,' she said in a mocking tone while finding her footing again. 'I didn't know you had it in you, Gary!' Then she kicked out at Dad, hitting him just below the ribcage. He let out a sharp cry of pain.

'Dad!' screamed Peanut. 'Are you OK?' She knew how ruthless Nerys, or Mr White, could be, and that she wouldn't hesitate to push Dad from the building. Peanut was terrified of losing him again, having only just got him back.

'Don't worry about me,' he wheezed, before managing to reach up and grab Nerys's other ankle. He pulled and, again, she slipped. But somehow she managed to keep drawing. That said, the desperation on her face was clear for all to see.

'Now you're just being annoying,' Nerys said. She only needed to complete the bottom part of the door handle, then she'd be able to open the door and dive through it. Dad still had hold of her ankle, but if she had to take him with her, she would – a fact that was not lost on a nervous Peanut.

Dad knew that time was running out, and that this was his last chance to get the pencil. Summoning all his strength, he let go of Nerys, placed his hands on either side of the ladder, and propelled himself rapidly upwards. The top of his head hit Nerys's right elbow hard, forcing her hand to open.

Little Tail flew straight up into the air.

Nerys snatched at it but missed completely. Dad, on the

other hand, maintained a laser focus. As the spinning pencil fell back down through the air, he reached out.

And then, for the very first time, Gary Jones's fingers closed around Pencil Number One.

64
The Prophecy

Nothing happened.

No fireworks. No explosions. No ribbons of colour.

'Dad!' shouted Peanut from below. 'Are you OK?'

'Er, yes,' he mumbled. 'I, er, I have the pencil, but I . . . I don't . . . The prophecy said . . .'

He was in total shock.

Nerys seized her chance. She snatched the pencil back from Dad's left hand and bounded up the ladder, stamping hard on the fingers of his right hand as she climbed. Dad howled in pain, lost his grip and tumbled to the bottom of the mast, taking Peanut with him.

Mum screamed. Little-Bit, Rockwell and Leo ran to help them.

Nerys, meanwhile, had hauled herself onto a small, circular platform at the very top of the ladder. Slowly, she stood up, lifted the pencil and continued drawing the door in the air.

'Peanut! Are you OK?' said Rockwell. But he didn't get an answer.

Instead, Peanut jumped to her feet, squeezed past him and started to climb the ladder as quickly as she could.

But it was too late.

Nerys had already finished the drawing.

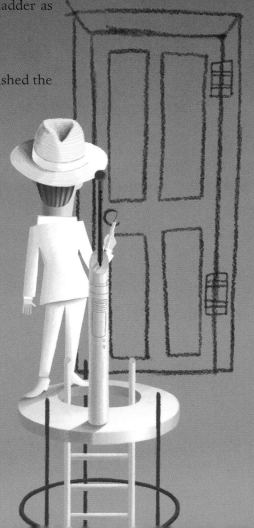

65

Vincent van Gogh

Peanut watched helplessly as Nerys reached out and turned the illustrated handle. The latch clicked and she pushed the door. On the other side of the threshold, Peanut could see the oak-panelled walls of the Blood, Stone & Partners offices in London.

'I must say, Peanut,' said Nerys, looking over her shoulder as she stepped through, 'that you have been a worthy adversary. You *nearly* managed to stop me. I'll admit that you have a very creative brain, lovely. It's just a shame that the world will never get to see your artistic talents. They'll just have to make do with mine, I suppose.'

'VINCENT VAN GOGH!' shouted Peanut, as loudly and dramatically as she could.

Nerys stopped. She turned around, half-in and half-out of the doorway.

'I beg your pardon, lovely?'

'Er, Vincent van Gogh!' Peanut repeated, desperately trying to organise her thoughts as the wind whipped around her head. 'Back when he was painting, people thought he was a terrible artist. In fact, they laughed at his work. They said it was rubbish, and they said it so many times that he ended up believing them. Vincent van Gogh considered himself a total failure! Can you believe that? Did you know that he only ever sold one painting in his lifetime?'

'What's that got to do with anything?' asked Nerys, confused.

Peanut wasn't sure why, but, again, she felt she had to keep Nerys talking. She swallowed hard and continued, 'It's just that . . . everything you're trying to do, everything you have been doing, all stems from the fact that you think that you've failed. As an artist, I mean.'

'Failed?'

'Because you didn't get into the Royal College all those years ago,' replied Peanut, her mouth dry. 'That's where this all started, right?'

'Yes, well, I'll show them!' said Nerys, the muscles in her jaw clenching. 'Let's see if they still think my style is too naïve, shall we? Once I'm the only artist in the world, they'll *have* to appreciate my talents!'

'You see,' said Peanut, 'that's my point. Why do you care what other people think? You shouldn't need anybody to tell you whether you're good or not. If you enjoy painting and creating, then that's enough. You *are* good at it. If you decide you want to be an artist, then you *are* an artist.'

Nerys frowned.

'Look,' continued Peanut, 'if van Gogh had listened to all those people back in the day and decided to give up, we wouldn't have his beautiful paintings to enjoy today. The fact is he *didn't* give up. He carried on. Because, for him, the creation of the art *was* the point of it. Not what other people thought of it.'

Nerys took a small step forward, back towards Chroma.

'And who gets to decide what's good and what's bad anyway?' asked Peanut. 'It's all a matter of personal taste, isn't it? With art, there is no right answer and there is no wrong answer. It's not like maths.' She glanced down at Rockwell as she said the last part. 'That's the beauty of it. *Everyone* can draw. *Everyone* can paint. And if you enjoy it, then that's all that matters.'

Nerys didn't say anything.

Peanut smiled. 'Just because one person didn't think you were good enough to get into the Royal College, it doesn't mean that you are a failure as an artist. That was just *one* decision taken in *one* moment by *one* individual. Maybe they were just having a bad day. Whatever it was, *please* don't punish all of us for one person's opinion.'

Peanut held her breath for a moment and crossed her fingers.

Nerys looked at the girl with an odd expression on

her face, like she was seeing her properly for the first time. She held up the pencil, looked at its long point and blinked three times . . . Then she took a step backwards.

'So many pretty words,' she said. 'You certainly paint a very nice picture with them. All complete nonsense, of course, but pretty words nevertheless. Now, it's time I went.'

Peanut's smile fell as Nerys backed through the door, waving.

'Goodbye, lovely. It's been—'

Nerys stopped talking. Something far below had caught her eye. Movement. A small, dark shape. A scribble of fur with legs and tail.

'Doodle!' shouted Little-Bit.

The illustrated dog had sprinted out onto the walkway and was running at full speed up the steps towards the mast. Suddenly, the large brown rat sitting on Doodle's back leapt onto the ladder and started to climb it at phenomenal speed. Before Nerys even had a chance to finish her goodbye, Woodhouse had reached the top, scurried up her white suit and knocked Little Tail out of her hand.

'Not so useless now, eh?' he said in his broad Glaswegian accent as the pencil flew high into the air.

WHACK!

66
The Fall

Everything moved in slow motion.

The pencil flew.

Up . . . up . . . up . . .

High above the mast.

Spinning . . .

Spinning . . .

Spinning . . .

Spinning . . .

Then it began to fall.

Tumbling . . .

twirling . . .

round and round . . .

Past peanut . . .

Past Nerys . . .

336

Down . . .

down . . .

down . . .

It would surely break

when it hit the ground,

trapping them all

in Chroma

forever.

Then a hand shot out

and grabbed it.

67

Prophecy, Fulfilled

Leo stood on the walkway holding the pencil in his right hand. The moment he caught it, a warm tingling sensation spread from the tips of his fingers to the palm of his hand. Then it moved up his arm and flooded his entire body. Every hair follicle, every blood vessel, every skin pore and every nerve ending fizzed.

It was happening.

Something made him lift his arm high above his head and point the pencil at the sky.

It was time.

A torrent of colour flew from the long, sharp graphite point of Pencil Number One with the combined explosive force of every firework that had ever been lit. Swirling, twisting

ribbons of red, green, pink, yellow, blue, orange and purple filled the sky, its blank canvas welcoming the multicoloured eruption like the desert welcomes rain. Teal, indigo, magenta, violet. Crimson, lavender, maroon, butterscotch. The heavens were painted with rainbows.

'WHAT'S HAPPENING?' shouted a terrified Nerys. She jumped back onto the small, circular platform as her illustrated door began to disintegrate.

Peanut's face danced with colour, the joyous scene reflected in her wide eyes as she tried to take in the magnificence of what was happening in front of her.

'It's Leo,' she whispered, as bronze, silver and gold starbursts lit up the city. '*Leo* is Conté's heir.'

68
Colour

O f course!' shouted Dad, as he stood proudly watching his son conduct the orchestra of colour playing its symphony over Chroma. 'The moment Leo turned eighteen, he automatically became Conté's heir!'

The citizens on the ground, who'd been trapped in the Rainbow Lake, looked up in wonder as the huge technicolour curtain drifted down towards them. As it passed over the Spire, jets of ink, paint and dye whizzed around it, dancing and exploding, scattering their beauty and decorating its facade.

'This is WONDERFUL!' shouted Mum, as she hugged Little-Bit and Rockwell while the colours passed over them.

Woodhouse had scurried back down the ladder as quickly

as he had scurried up it and had now resumed his position on Doodle's back. Both illustrated animals wagged their tails wildly.

'Doodle! Woodhouse!' shouted Peanut from her position near the top of the ladder. 'You made this happen! You saved us all!'

'Totally!' agreed Little-Bit. 'Woodhouse, I don't know how you escaped from that horrid snake, but I'm so glad you did!'

'Me too!' said a gleeful Rockwell. 'After today, I will never look at rodents in the same way. Three cheers for Woodhouse and Doodle! Hip, hip . . .'

'HOORAY!' chorused everyone.

'Hip, hip . . .'

'HOORAY!'

'Hip, hip . . .'

'HOORAY!'

Doodle yipped with delight. Woodhouse would have blushed if rats could, indeed, blush. Instead, he stood up straight and waved his long tail elegantly behind him. He *had* saved the day. He, a small creature who most people thought of as lowly and dirty, had saved Chroma and – what's more – the entire world's creativity! His tail curled into the shape of an open palm and he accepted enthusiastic high-fives from everyone there.

Meanwhile, the technicolour display continued to dazzle in the sky. Then, the most remarkable thing happened. When the curtain of colour reached the ground, the lake, totally empty of citizens by now, began to refill with rainbow-coloured water. The liquid tumbled and splashed as it magically poured into the lake, its surface gradually rising until it lapped playfully at the brim. Once there, the water settled into its familiar striped pattern that the children had seen on their first visit to the city.

'Perfect,' whispered Rockwell, looking down on the newly restored rings of colour. 'Everything is back to how it should be.'

And with that, the entire city, revelling in this wonderful eruption of colour and creation, of light and life, of chaos and magic, breathed a huge sigh of relief.

69
The Nerys Balloon

eanut!' shouted Leo from his position several metres below her on the walkway. 'Grab the balloon!'

'What balloon?' she cried.

'There!' Leo pointed.

A perplexed Nerys was suspended in the centre of a huge multicoloured bubble which was floating just above the small, circular platform at the top of the ladder. Attached to the bubble was a long piece of string, the end of which was dangling near Peanut's right hand.

'How did you do that?' she asked Leo.

'I . . . I . . . don't know. I just thought it would be a good idea to trap her in some way, and then this jet of magical

stuff came out of Little Tail, shot towards Nerys and made this happen!'

'Ah,' Peanut said, smiling. 'The power of the pencil and the artist who wields it.'

'The power of what?' asked Leo, looking very confused.

'Oh, never mind.'

Carefully, Peanut climbed down the ladder, towing the Nerys balloon behind her, and happily embraced everybody on the walkway.

'Peanut, I think this is yours,' said Leo, offering her the pencil.

'No,' she said. 'You're Conté's true heir. It belongs to you.'

'Peanut, I don't care about any ancient rules or inheritances. It's obvious to everybody that the pencil should stay with you. It's practically an extension of your body!'

She paused for a second, then took it from her brother.

'Well, if you're sure,' she said, turning it slowly in her hands. 'I must admit, it's nice to have it back.'

A small shower of colourful sparkles burst from the pencil's tip.

'I think Little Tail is happy to be reunited with you too,' said Rockwell, laughing.

70
The Quick Way Down

'Is everybody ready?' asked Peanut, standing right next to the opening she'd made in the walkway's barrier.

'YES!' replied Little-Bit, Rockwell, Doodle, Woodhouse, Leo, Mum and Dad in unison. Each of them was holding a beautifully illustrated skateboard.

'In that case, MOUNT YOUR BOARDS!' shouted Peanut as the wind blew through her topknot.

Everybody put their skateboards down and stood on them carefully, holding onto each other for balance. Then Peanut held the can of spray paint in front of her, pointed it just ahead of her board, and pushed the button. A wide blast of rainbow-coloured paint came flying out of the nozzle, creating a length of runway in front of them that was angled downwards like a ramp. Confidently, Peanut dropped onto it and began skating. One by one, each member of the group followed, some more confidently than others. As they descended, Nerys floated above them in the colourful bubble now being towed by Dad. She looked thoroughly dejected.

This wasn't Peanut's first rodeo. As she sprayed the curved runway circling the Spire, she remembered the first time she'd descended it in this fashion. Today, however, things looked very different.

As Chroma rotated below them, the incredible views were made even more breathtaking by the effect that Leo's colour explosion was having on the city. A multicoloured cloud radiated out from the Spire, restoring happiness and life to everything that had been mono-ed by Nerys. The Ink District, The Strip, The Light District, Vincent Fields, Die Brücke, Modernia, The Grid, Cubeside, Warholia, Dalí Point West and The Green Valleys all looked brand new once the cloud had passed over them. Iridescent, colourful, splendid.

The North Draw showed the biggest change, since it was the first district that Nerys had targeted and, therefore,

the worst affected. Peanut stared in wonder from her bird's-eye view as the magic moved slowly over the bleak snowfields, leaving lush, green meadows in its wake.

As she led the group down towards the ground, Peanut's thoughts were filled with every single adventure that Rockwell, Little-Bit and she had had since they first arrived in Chroma. She smiled to herself. Even though many of these adventures had been quite scary at the time, she knew that she wouldn't change a thing. Well, maybe she'd rethink the whole falling out with Rockwell part, but aside from that . . .

With perfect timing, a loud fluttering sound and a sudden rush of air signalled the arrival of some old friends. The three magnificent kaleidoscoppi that she'd set free from Mr White's cages during their first visit to the city had arrived to accompany the gang on their final descent.

'What beautiful creatures,' said Mum, awestruck.

That was their cue. The three birds began to sing, in perfect harmony, the most bewitching melody that any of them had ever heard in their lives.

In that moment, Peanut knew one thing for sure: that she had grown to love this city more than she ever thought possible. And that whatever happened in the future, no matter where life took her, she would always carry a little bit of it with her. Right there. In her heart.

71
The Joys of Spring

A few minutes later, they reached the bottom of the spray-painted skateboard ramp and landed on the crowded concrete expanse at the bottom of the Spire, which was now dotted with blooming flowers and blossoming shrubbery.

'THERE THEY ARE!'

Mr and Mrs Markmaker rushed over to greet the group, their feet still covered with plaster. As they skipped through the daffodils, snowdrops and tulips, they somehow looked twenty years younger. They were, quite literally, full of the joys of spring.

'CAN YOU BELIEVE IT?' shouted Mr M. 'Look at the

lake! Look at the Spire! Look at the city! Everything is back to how it was when I was a boy! This has all turned out better than we could ever have hoped!'

'I've never been so happy!' chirruped Mrs M. 'Even before 67 trapped us all in the lake, we thought it would take years to restore Chroma to its former glory. But now look at it! It's more beautiful than it's ever been!'

'Did you see what just happened?' asked Mr M, excitedly. 'It was just like the stories my parents used to tell me about Conté and his ribbons of colour. I don't know who was responsible for that explosion of colour, but, if I were a betting man, I'd put a lot of money on it being you, Peanut.'

'Actually, it was L—' Peanut began to say.

'It was all of us,' interrupted Leo. 'A true team effort.'

'And *what* a team you make!' beamed Mrs M. 'The best there's ever been!'

The Resistance leader turned around to call to the throng of operatives, who were celebrating on the flower-strewn concrete. 'Everyone – come over here! Look who I found!'

'72!' yelled a delighted Little-Bit as the robot, whose eyes were currently displaying as bright pink hearts, approached. 'You look fab!'

Doodle, meanwhile, had jumped up onto Jonathan Higginbottom's tail and run along the entire length of his

body before covering the alligator's long snout with a thick layer of doggy slobber.

'ROCKWELL!' shouted Josephine as she dashed over to greet her young apprentice.

'Josephine!' he replied, eagerly. 'Tell me, tell me, tell me! How did you do it? How did you stop the Giant X and get everybody out of the lake before it filled with plaster?'

'It was actually quite simple,' she replied. 'I just used the same technology that 67 did to gain control of the RAZER army in the first place. I overrode their protocol, forced the exocetia out of their little holes and back across the lake with their steel cables, which allowed everyone to get out. Then I ordered the RAZERs piloting the Giant X to turn their taps off and land safely in the North Draw. Oh, and I also reversed the paralysis of the RAZERs you incapacitated with my device. With a little bit of clever programming, I've even managed to turn them all to our side. Even 67.'

'I KNEW IT!' shouted Rockwell, turning to Peanut. 'Didn't I say that's what she would have done? Didn't I say that, Peanut?'

'You did,' Peanut laughed.

'Well, I had a lot of help from these guys, too,' said Josephine, nodding to her right.

The superheroes stood in a long, curved line, like the cast of an extremely bizarre pantomime about to take their final bow. They had somehow managed to arrange themselves so that they were beautifully backlit with their hair caught perfectly on the breeze. Every single one of them had adopted a dynamic hands-on-hips stance, which allowed their cloaks to billow out heroically behind them.

Table Guy stepped forward and spoke to Peanut.

'Citizen! We stand here today humbled by your magnificent and selfless contribution to Chroma's long and courageous struggle against tyranny! To the ongoing battle of good versus evil, freedom versus oppression, light versus shade!' He stared into the middle distance. 'This may be your victory, but it belongs to each and every one of us! Throughout history, our trials, tribulations and struggles have been met by an unbending resolve, which has—'

The superhero was stopped, mid-speech, by Woodhouse who had zipped along the floor and climbed up his cloak.

'Och, you're a lovely fella,' said the rat, laughing, 'But you don't half talk a lot!' Then he planted a big, wet, rodenty kiss on Table Guy.

'Hang on a second,' said Mr M. 'Is that . . . Mr White? There in that . . . balloon? How did he get in there?'

The entire crowd looked up at the forlorn figure inside the sphere floating on the end of the piece of string that Dad was still holding.

'It is,' said Peanut.

'But . . . if that's Mr White,' said Mrs M, 'who's this?'

A bedraggled, plaster-splattered Mr Stone was brought out from behind the throng of superheroes by Cheese Girl, who had bound his wrists with a particularly stretchy variety of mozzarella.

'For the last time,' shouted Stone, 'I have no idea who this White chap is. He is not me and I am not him! If it's any consolation, I think he sounds pretty dreadful. But, as I keep saying, he has absolutely nothing to do with me!'

'He's right,' said Peanut. 'Stone isn't White. He's just my mum's slightly annoying boss. No more, no less. You should probably set him free.'

'But if *he's* not Mr White, who is?' asked a confused Mr M.

Gary pulled the balloon down to the ground and Peanut popped it with Little Tail's sharp point. Nerys immediately tried to run, but Leo and Dad grabbed her arms. Peanut lifted the fedora from her head.

'NERYS?' exclaimed an astonished Mr Stone. 'What are you doing with my hat? And where the devil did you get that suit? Although, I must say, it's pretty dashing. Beautiful cut. Can you give me your tailor's details?'

Peanut shook her head in disbelief. The Markmakers looked equally bewildered.

'Oh, put a sock in it, Stone,' shouted Nerys. 'You are, and always have been, an awful boss. Making everybody think that *you* were the person who wanted to rid the world of its creativity was the least you deserved.'

'Charming!' he replied.

'And what's more,' she continued, 'I'd like to hand in my notice!'

'Well, I don't accept,' said Stone, smiling to reveal a set of perfect white teeth. 'Because, actually, I've already decided to sack you.' He pointed a thick finger directly at her face. 'Nerys, you're fired!' he said, with gusto.

'Ooh, it's all happening today, isn't it?' said Mrs M. 'I tell you what, why don't we pop indoors and I'll make us all a nice cup of hot chocolate. Then, Peanut, you can tell us everything.'

The Door

'Are you sure *you* don't want to do this, Peanut?' asked Leo nervously, as he did his best to draw a door with Little Tail.

'I'm sure,' she replied. 'You're Conté's heir. You should at least have a go. Remember to think of our house as you draw it. Get a really clear picture of it in your head and concentrate on the reasons why you want to go there. The pencil should pick up on all that stuff, and then the door will take us to the right place.'

'OK,' he replied, before repeating the phrase, *There's no place like home, there's no place like home, there's no place like home . . .* several times.

'All right, Dorothy,' said Rockwell. 'Get a shift on, will you?

If we're quick, I can probably still make it home in time for dinner. Also, some of us have got physics revision to do!'

'Oh, well there's a surprise,' said Peanut, laughing. 'Rockwell's worrying about his homework!'

When he had finally finished, Leo stepped back to look at his sketch.

'It's very good,' said Mum.

'It really is,' agreed Dad. 'We'll make an artist out of you yet, Leonardo.'

Little-Bit gently tugged at the bottom of Peanut's bandolier. 'We will come back one day, won't we?' she asked quietly. 'And will everyone here in Chroma be OK without us?'

'*Of course* we'll be back, LB!' said Peanut, putting an arm round her sister's shoulder. 'Listen, the Markmakers are in charge now, so there's nothing to worry about. And they've got Josephine, 72 and Jonathan Higginbottom to help them. You heard what Mrs M said. That she's dead set on rehabilitating Nerys in prison. She's confident that she can instil her with the true values of art. If anyone can do it, Mrs M can. And don't forget that Table Guy and his buddies are always on hand over in Superhero Heights should they ever need more help. So don't worry.'

'And what happens if you grow up and don't ever want to go back to Chroma?' asked Little-Bit.

'Well, firstly, that won't happen,' said Peanut. 'But,

regardless of what *I* do, *you* can visit whenever you want. The twelve portals have already been reopened, so you don't need Little Tail or me to visit.'

Little-Bit smiled. She seemed happy with the answer.

'Right,' said Peanut. 'Where were we?'

She looked at Leo's drawing of the door.

'Ah, yes. Go on then, Leo. Open it. It's time for us to go home.'

Leo grabbed the handle. It felt cold, as if it were made of brass rather than graphite. He rotated it a quarter-turn anti-clockwise. Something clicked.

And then the door opened . . .

One Year Later...

Little-Bit pushed the hatch.

It opened with a loud creak and a shower of dust drifted down onto her forehead. She wiped it away and hauled herself into the attic.

It smelled exactly like the old bike shed at school, the one that no one ever used because they thought a troll lived in it. A pungent mixture of damp wood and old sock. It was also very dark up there. The one shard of pale light that had fought its way in through a small window in the sloping ceiling wasn't doing its job very well. *How am I supposed to find the sewing machine in these conditions?* she thought.

She walked around the musty room looking for

something with the word *SINGER* written on it. Ever since the Markmakers had told Peanut and her that the new-and-improved Nerys had become an exceptional quilt-maker while in prison back in Chroma, Little-Bit had been determined to give sewing a try herself. When Mum mentioned that Auntie Jean had a machine that Gran had left for her when she'd died, Little-Bit decided to try to find it. She didn't realise that she'd have to brave the dreaded attic to do so, however.

She was in the darkest corner of the room, rummaging through a pile of old *Just Seventeen* magazines, when she found something curious hidden beneath an issue with a young Leonardo DiCaprio on the cover. It was a flat, green leather case, with a small handle and tarnished brass hinges and clasps. It looked very old, its surface peeling and flaking around the reinforced corners.

Little-Bit picked it up. Then she walked over to the shard of pale light, knelt on the floor and put the case on her lap. It was much heavier than she had expected it to be.

She pressed the two clasps with her thumbs and they flipped open with a satisfying *thunk*. Slowly, she opened the lid.

Inside were three of the most beautiful objects that Little-Bit had ever seen, each one solid silver, highly polished and elaborately ornamented. It was a musical instrument of some sort and, to her eyes, it looked brand new. But it couldn't have been. The case was ancient. And it was buried under loads of old magazines. It must have been up in the attic for years.

'It's a flute,' she said aloud, when she noticed the lip-plate. 'Just like the one Marley uses in Junior Orchestra, but a lot cleaner.'

She picked up the long, gleaming barrel and the smaller foot joint and slotted them together. She then inserted the neck piece into the other end. As she did so, a single exquisite harmonic rang out.

Little-Bit smiled. She had never played a flute before, but something compelled her to try to get a tune out of this one. She lifted the lip-plate to her mouth and held the instrument out to the side, like she'd seen Marley do at school. Then she took a deep breath and blew.

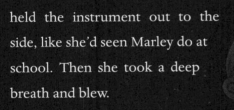

Suddenly, her fingers began to dance across the keys and, to her complete surprise, the most beautiful melody filled the room. Little-Bit almost dropped the flute with shock. *How did that happen?* she wondered.

And then she saw it.

A thin, vertical strip of white light had appeared in the opposite corner of the attic. It seemed to be . . . floating in mid-air. Little-Bit stood up and walked towards it. As she got closer, she saw that it was some sort of . . . rip. A tear in space, almost.

She blinked hard and slapped her cheeks with both hands to make sure she wasn't dreaming. Then she lifted the flute to her mouth, took another deep breath and blew again. This time, the tune was even more beautiful than it had been before. She continued to play, and as she did so, the rip got wider. And wider. Soon it had become a hole, big enough for her to climb through. Little-Bit recognised what it was. She, of all people, knew a portal when she saw one.

She moved closer to the rip and looked through. On the other side was a bright white landscape that looked like it was made entirely of light. On the floor was a pathway comprised of five thick, parallel lines which led to a large wooden sign. Little-Bit squinted, but she couldn't quite make out what the words on it said. She needed to

Perhaps the decision had already been made for her, or perhaps she made it herself, there and then. Either way, Little-Bit stepped through the portal and walked along the path towards the sign. Five steps later, she could read the words clearly. And when she did, she found herself at the beginning of a whole new adventure.

About the author

Rob Biddulph is a bestselling and multi award-winning author/illustrator whose books include *Blown Away, Odd Dog Out, Kevin* and *Show and Tell*. In March 2020 he started *#DrawWithRob*, a series of draw-along videos designed to help parents whose children were forced to stay home from school due to the coronavirus pandemic. The initiative garnered widespread international media coverage and millions of views across the globe. On 21 May 2020 he broke the Guinness World Record for the largest online art class when 45,611 households tuned in to his live *#DrawWithRob* YouTube class, and in July 2020 he was named as a Point of Light by the Prime Minister. He lives in London with his wife and daughters, Ringo the dog and Catface the cat. He is, for his sins, an Arsenal fan.

Glossary

Banksy

Banksy's real identity is a mystery but he is believed to be British. As a graffiti artist, he uses public walls as a canvas and stencils and spray paint to create his designs quickly. His works usually appear overnight and are often cheeky comments on contemporary society. Banksy's art sells for millions. This often means that people buy and remove the entire wall it was painted on!

Hieronymus Bosch (1450—1516)

Hieronymus Bosch was a Dutch oil painter. Bosch's most famous paintings are triptychs (three pictures that make up one image when put together) painted on large wooden panels. His paintings are very detailed and often feature religious imagery.

Michelangelo Merisi da Caravaggio (1571—1610)

Caravaggio was an Italian painter whose art came to influence many other artists and artistic movements. He worked in Rome, Sicily and Malta, and was famous for his dramatic, almost theatrical use of light.

Church of Santa Maria delle Grazie

The Santa Maria delle Grazie is a gothic style church in Milan, Northern Italy. It is famously the place where Leonardo da Vinci painted his mural *The Last Supper*.

Nicolas-Jacques Conté (1755–1805)

Nicolas-Jacques Conté was born in Normandy, France, and is the inventor of the modern pencil. He was also an artist and produced many portraits from which he made a lot of his money.

Salvador Dalí (1904–1989)

Salvador Dalí was an important surrealist painter and printmaker born in Figueres, Spain. He is perhaps most famous for creating the Mae West Lips Sofa and for his painting *The Persistence of Memory* (1931), which is considered one of the masterpieces of the twentieth century.

Marcel Duchamp (1887–1968)

Marcel Duchamp was a French artist whose work is often assciated with the surrealist movement. He is famous for exhibiting his 'ready mades', which were objects that already existed, like a bicycle wheel and a urinal. He did this to prove that anything can be considered art.

Joseph Engelberger (1925–2015)

Josephine Engelberger, designer and inventor of the RAZERs, is inspired by the real-life Joseph Engelberger, who was an American engineer born in Brooklyn, New York, in 1925. He is most famous for his contribution to automated production lines and is today considered the 'father of robotics'.

The Jinou Yonggu Cup

The Jinou Yonggu Cup, which translates into English as the 'Cup of Solid Gold', belonged to the Emperor Qianlong, and was created in 1739 as a birthday present to him. The cup is made of gold, pearls and diamonds, and is one of the greatest treasures of the so-called 'Forbidden City' in Beijing.

The Last Supper and *Mona Lisa* — Leonardo da Vinci

The Last Supper and *Mona Lisa* are two of Leonardo da Vinci's best-known works. The *Mona Lisa* is a small painting that can be seen in the Louvre, Paris. The *Last Supper* is a mural depicting Jesus and his twelve apostles at the exact moment that Jesus announces that one of his apostles will betray him. It can be found on the refectory wall at the Santa Maria delle Grazie church in Milan.

L. S. Lowry (1887–1976)

L. S. Lowry is most famous for his paintings of everyday life in the industrial areas of North West England. He developed a very distinctive style of painting, using drab colours, and his human figures were often referred to as 'matchstick men'.

William MacGillivray (1796—1852)

William MacGillivray was a famous Scottish naturalist and ornithologist (an expert on birds). He created more than 200 important watercolour paintings of animals, many of which can be found at the Natural History Museum in London.

Queen Victoria — Sir Joseph Edgar Boehm

The Queen Victoria bust mentioned in the story was made by Sir Joseph Edgar Boehm, a sculptor born in Vienna, in 1834. He moved to London in 1848, and is most famous for creating the coinage portrait of the so-called 'Jubilee head' of Queen Victoria in 1887. He was also known for creating portrait busts, many of which can be seen in the National Portrait Gallery in London.

The Scream — Edvard Munch

The Scream is Edvard Munch's most iconic and well known composition. It depicts an androgynous, human-like figure screaming beneath a red sky, and is said to be an expression of anxiety and fear. The idea for the work came to Munch when out walking at sunset. He said that the clouds turned 'blood red' and he sensed an 'infinite scream passing through nature'.

Vincent van Gogh (1853—1890)

Vincent van Gogh was born in the Netherlands and is one of history's most influential artists. He used bold colours and short, expressive brush-strokes. His best-known paintings include *Van Gogh's Chair* and *Starry Night*. He is also famous for cutting his own ear off!

Water Lilies — Claude Monet

Born in France, Monet (1840–1926) was interested in nature and the French countryside. He liked to paint the same scene over and over again, observing how its appearance changed throughout the day due to the changing light. He is probably best known for 'Water Lilies', a series of approximately 250 paintings depicting his garden in Giverny, France.

9018411914

Please return/renew this item by the last date shown.
Item may also be renewed by the internet*

https://library.eastriding.gov.uk

* Please note a PIN will be required to access this service
- this can be obtained from your library.